THE SANTA CLAUS STORIES

THE SANTA CLAUS
STORIES

L. FRANK BAUM

WFP
WordFire Press

The Santa Claus Stories

L. Frank Baum

Foreword by Dean Wesley Smith
Introduction by James Romag
This compilation © 2020 WordFire Press
Original publication information listed at end of book

EBook ISBN: 978-1-68057-103-5
Trade Paperback ISBN: 978-1-68057-102-8
Hardcover ISBN: 978-1-68057-104-2

Edited by James Romag
Cover design by James Romag and Janet McDonald
Cover artwork image by Mary Cowles Clark, from *The Life and Adventures of Santa Claus*

Published by
WordFire Press, LLC
PO Box 1840
Monument CO 80132
Kevin J. Anderson & Rebecca Moesta, Publishers
WordFire Press eBook Edition 2020
WordFire Press Trade Paperback Edition 2020
WordFire Press Hardcover Edition 2020
Printed in the USA
Join our WordFire Press Readers Group for
sneak previews, updates, new projects, and giveaways.
Sign up at wordfirepress.com

CONTENTS

A KIDNAPPED SANTA CLAUS

(EXCERPT FROM) THE ROAD TO OZ

HOW THE WOGGLEBUG AND HIS FRIENDS VISITED SANTA CLAUS

FOREWORD

DEAN WESLEY SMITH

James Romag is the editor of this fantastic volume of stories from the master storyteller L. Frank Baum. And James has done an amazing job bringing back to light some lost works of a great author who was responsible for so much cultural history that so many of us just take for granted.

When you mention to someone that L. Frank Baum had a major influence on the holiday of Christmas we now celebrate, that person will just look at you with a puzzled expression. In this single volume, James has done a service for all of us by bringing Baum's fantastic Christmas stories together for, as far as I know, the first time ever.

This book will be a treasure for you and something to read to your children during the holidays.

Now, let me have James Romag explain the history of Baum's stories and why this book is so important to our modern culture. So read and enjoy all the wonderful stories. I know I sure did.

Dean Wesley Smith is a USA Today bestselling American author who's published more than 200 novels and hundreds of short stories in mystery, fantasy, science fiction, and multiple other genres. During his career, Dean also wrote a couple dozen Star Trek *novels, the only two original* Men in Black *novels, and* Spider-Man *and* X-Men *novels, plus novels set in gaming and television worlds. He can be found at deanwesleysmith.com.*

INTRODUCTION

JAMES ROMAG

Known the world over for his Land of Oz series, American author Lyman Frank Baum was equally successful penning other fantasy tales for children. Well over a century ago, Baum sat down and wrote a handful of narratives that not only entertained in the moment but lived on and helped forge our collective popular image of the legend known as Santa Claus.

There were other American authors, of course, who wrote of Santa, or Saint Nicholas, before Baum took his turn. Washington Irving mentioned St. Nicholas in his 1809 satire piece "Knickerbocker's History of New York." In "History," Irving includes a brief passage regarding St. Nicholas, who "came riding over the tops of the trees, in that self-same wagon wherein he brings his yearly presents to children." When it was time to leave, St. Nicholas lay "his finger beside his nose" and returned over the treetops. Little else is said of St. Nicholas in "History," however, and Irving's 1876 "Old Christmas" makes no mention of Saint Nicholas at all.

Clement Clarke Moore (or perhaps it was Henry Livingston, Jr.) drafted "A Visit from St. Nicholas" in 1823. That holiday poem, as everyone knows, gave us a chubby and plump St. Nick driving a miniature sleigh with eight tiny reindeer on his travels to fill children's stockings hung by the chimney.

But it was Baum's pen that really captivated our imagination and shaped our modern impression of Santa Claus. Beginning with his "Little Bun Rabbit" short story from *Mother Goose in Prose* in 1897, Baum tells of Santa and his reindeer taking toys to children on a miraculous journey around the world in a single night, arriving back home before dawn.

In 1902's *The Life and Adventures of Santa Claus*, Baum recounts the full tale of Santa, from his abandonment in the Forest of Burzee and subsequent adoption by a wood-nymph named Necile, to his visits on the cities of mankind where he saw the suffering of the children and vowed to make them happy, to his growing old, heavy, and gray before being granted immortality.

Life and Adventures explains how Claus got his name: "... let him be called Neclaus ... for that will mean 'Necile's little one.'" From Neclaus came Nicklaus or Nicolas, "which is the reason that Santa Claus is still known in some lands as St. Nicolas." It's also in *Life and Adventures* where we witness Claus making his first toy of many—carving a cat from wood—and eventually becoming the Patron Saint of Children, or Santa Claus.

Baum's lasting voice filled our heads with the sound of sleigh bells and thoughts of reindeer pulling a sledge full of toys for children, with visions of the old fellow making his way down chimneys to drop gifts into stockings hung by the fireplace, and with the echo of Santa calling out, "Ho, ho, ho!" as he carried out his duties. Baum told us how Santa brought Christmas trees to so many homes and why he deputized parents to help him on Christmas eve, all in his quest to bring joy to children around the world.

As the short story "A Kidnapped Santa Claus" from 1904 shows us, nothing can stop Santa's good will. When he's taken by Daemons, his immortal friends—a Ryl, a Knook, a Pixie, and a Fairy—take up Santa's mission to make children happy and deliver his toys, though not without a few mistakes.

Further solidifying the modern image of Santa, when he visits Princess Ozma for her birthday in 1909's *The Road to Oz*, Baum describes him as "round as an apple, with a fresh rosy face, laughing eyes, and a bushy beard as white as snow," with a "red cloak trimmed with beautiful ermine."

To be sure, not all of Baum's work has become lore. In "Little Bun Rabbit," Santa lived atop a mountain in a castle of gold and silver with windows made of diamond where Mother Hubbard served his meals. In other tales, Santa lived in the Laughing Valley of Hohaho and had ten reindeer pulling his sledge each year. Those reindeer, by the way, never flew, but traveled swiftly in great leaps. And with nary an elf in sight in any of the stories, Santa made all the toys himself, though he did have help from some fairies getting toys into any houses without proper chimneys.

Baum's classic holiday tales have rightfully endured for more than a hundred years and those five stories are now collected in one volume, the appropriately titled *The Santa Claus Stories of L. Frank Baum*, to be enjoyed any time of the year. Here's to those ten reindeer—Flossie and Glossie, Racer and Pacer, Reckless and Speckless, Fearless and Peerless, and Ready and Steady—and to anyone who's ever believed in Santa Claus.

Special thanks to Marcus Mebes from The International Wizard of Oz Club (ozclub.org) and Chris Glasgow, curator of the Oz Museum (ozmuseum.com), for their assistance in this compilation.

Santa Claus was good to me—
Gave me lots of things
Wrapped in dainty parcels
And tied with ribbon-strings.

I can't recall what lovely gifts
Within there chanced to be—
The wrappers and the ribbons
Were what are dear to me.

They breathe of sweet remembrance,
Of Love and Kindly Thought—
The things about my presents
That never could be bought.

And so, although I'm far away,
Love's message spans the space
And our two hearts are linked anew
Through dear old Santa's grace.

Untitled poem by L. Frank Baum, written to his sister, Mary Louise Brewster, published posthumously in Jack Snow's authorized *The Shaggy Man of Oz*.

LITTLE BUN RABBIT

ILLUSTRATED BY MAXFIELD PARRISH

"Little Bun Rabbit" first appeared in *1897's* Mother Goose in Prose.

EDITOR'S NOTE: The complete Mother Goose in Prose *consists of twenty-two children's short stories based on Mother Goose nursery rhymes. The final piece in the original collection is "Little Bun Rabbit," providing Santa's first appearance in Baum's stories. "Little Bun Rabbit" includes a character named Dorothy, but this is not the same Dorothy who later came to be known in the Land of Oz series. When "Little Bun Rabbit" was reprinted in his* Juvenile Speaker *in 1910, Baum changed the name to Doris to avoid confusion with Oz's Dorothy Gale.*

To the extent possible, the text of this story, to include spellings such as "good bye," is left as Baum originally wrote it.

୧୧୧୧୧

"I HAVE THOUGHT the children might like the (Mother Goose) stories told at greater length, that they may dwell longer upon their favorite heroes and heroines.

"For that reason I have written this book.

"In making the stories I have followed mainly the suggestions of the rhymes, and my hope is that the little ones will like them, and not find that they interfere with the fanciful creations of their own imaginations."

—*L. Frank Baum*
Chicago, Illinois
From the introduction to Mother Goose in Prose

Little Bun Rabbit

"Oh, Little Bun Rabbit, so soft and so shy,
"Say, what do you see with your big, round eye?"
"On Christmas we rabbits," says Bunny so shy,
"Keep watch to see Santa go galloping by."

LITTLE DOROTHY HAD PASSED ALL the few years of her life in the country, and being the only child upon the farm she was allowed to roam about the meadows and woods as she pleased. On the bright summer mornings Dorothy's mother would tie a sun-bonnet under the girl's chin, and then she romped away to the fields to amuse herself in her own way.

She came to know every flower that grew, and to call them by name, and she always stepped very carefully to avoid treading on them, for Dorothy was a kind-hearted child and did not like to crush the pretty flowers that bloomed in her path. And she was also very fond of all the animals, and learned to know them well, and even to understand their language, which very few people can do. And the animals loved

Dorothy in turn, for the word passed around amongst them that she could be trusted to do them no harm. For the horse, whose soft nose Dorothy often gently stroked, told the cow of her kindness, and the cow told the dog, and the dog told the cat, and the cat told her black kitten, and the black kitten told the rabbit when one day they met in the turnip patch.

Therefore when the rabbit, which is the most timid of all animals and the most difficult to get acquainted with, looked out of a small bush at the edge of the wood one day and saw Dorothy standing a little way off, he did not scamper away, as is his custom, but sat very still and met the gaze of her sweet eyes boldly, although perhaps his heart beat a little faster than usual.

Dorothy herself was afraid she might frighten him away, so she kept very quiet for a time, leaning silently against a tree and smiling encouragement at her timorous companion until the rabbit became reassured and blinked his big eyes at her thoughtfully. For he was as much interested in the little girl as she in him, since it was the first time he had dared to meet a person face to face.

Finally Dorothy ventured to speak, so she asked, very softly and slowly,

> *"Oh, Little Bun Rabbit, so soft and so shy,*
> *"Say, what do you see with your big, round eye?"*

"Many things," answered the rabbit, who was pleased to hear the girl speak in his own language; "in summer-time I see the clover-leaves that I love to feed upon and the cabbages at the end of the farmer's garden. I see the cool bushes where I can hide from my enemies, and I see the dogs and the men long before they can see me, or know that I am near, and therefore I am able to keep out of their way."

"Is that the reason your eyes are so big?" asked Dorothy.

"I suppose so," returned the rabbit; "you see we have only our eyes and our ears and our legs to defend ourselves with. We cannot fight, but we can always run away, and that is a much better way to save our lives than by fighting."

"Where is your home, bunny?" enquired the girl.

"I live in the ground, far down in a cool, pleasant hole I have dug in the midst of the forest. At the bottom of the hole is the nicest little room you can imagine, and there I have made a soft bed to rest in at night. When I meet an enemy I run to my hole and jump in, and there I stay until all danger is over."

"You have told me what you see in summer," continued Dorothy, who was greatly interested in the rabbit's account of himself, "but what do you see in the winter?"

> *"In winter we rabbits," said Bunny so shy,*
> *"Keep watch to see Santa go galloping by."*

"And do you ever see him?" asked the girl, eagerly.

"Oh, yes; every winter. I am not afraid of him, nor of his reindeer. And it is such fun to see him come dashing along, cracking his whip and calling out cheerily to his reindeer, who are able to run even swifter than we rabbits. And Santa Claus, when he sees me, always gives me a nod and a smile, and then I look after him and his big load of toys which he is carrying to the children, until he has galloped away out of sight. I like to see the toys, for they are so bright and pretty, and every year there is something new amongst them. Once I visited Santa, and saw him make the toys."

"Oh, tell me about it!" pleaded Dorothy.

"It was one morning after Christmas," said the rabbit, who seemed to enjoy talking, now that he had overcome his fear of Dorothy, "and I was sitting by the road-side when Santa Claus came riding back in his empty sleigh. He does not come home quite so fast as he goes, and when he saw me he stopped for a word.

"'You look very pretty this morning, Bun Rabbit,' he said, in his jolly way; 'I think the babies would love to have you to play with.'

"'I don't doubt it, your honor,' I answered; 'but they'd soon kill me with handling, even if they did not scare me to death; for babies are very rough with their playthings.'

"'That is true,' replied Santa Claus; 'and yet you are so soft and pretty it is a pity the babies can't have you. Still, as they would abuse a live rabbit I think I shall make them some toy rabbits, which they cannot hurt; so if you will jump into my sleigh with me and ride home to my castle for a few days, I'll see if I can't make some toy rabbits just like you.'

"Of course I consented, for we all like to please old Santa, and a minute later I had jumped into the sleigh beside him and we were dashing away at full speed toward his castle. I enjoyed the ride very much, but I enjoyed the castle far more; for it was one of the loveliest places you could imagine. It stood on the top of a high mountain and is built of gold and silver bricks, and the windows are pure diamond crystals. The rooms are big and high, and there is a soft carpet upon every floor and many strange things scattered around to amuse one. Santa Claus lives there all alone, except for old Mother Hubbard, who cooks the meals for him; and her cupboard is never bare now, I can promise you! At the top of the castle there is one big room, and that is Santa's work-shop, where he makes the toys. On one side is his work-bench, with plenty of saws and hammers and jack-knives; and on another side is the paint-bench, with paints of every color and brushes of every size and shape. And in other places are great shelves, where the toys are put to dry and keep new and bright until Christmas comes and it is time to load them all into his sleigh.

"After Mother Hubbard had given me a good dinner, and I

had eaten some of the most delicious clover I have ever tasted, Santa took me up into his work-room and sat me upon the table.

"'If I can only make rabbits half as nice as you are,' he said, 'the little ones will be delighted.' Then he lit a big pipe and began to smoke, and soon he took a roll of soft fur from a shelf in a corner and commenced to cut it out in the shape of a rabbit. He smoked and whistled all the time he was working, and he talked to me in such a jolly way that I sat perfectly still and allowed him to measure my ears and my legs so that he could cut the fur into the proper form.

"'Why, I've got your nose too long, Bunny,' he said once; and so he snipped a little off the fur he was cutting, so that the toy rabbit's nose should be like mine. And again he said, 'Good gracious! the ears are too short entirely!' So he had to get a needle and thread and sew on more fur to the ears, so that they might be the right size. But after a time it was all finished, and then he stuffed the fur full of sawdust and sewed it up neatly; after which he put in some glass eyes that made the toy rabbit look wonderfully life-like. When it was all done he put it on the table beside me, and at first I didn't know whether I was the live rabbit or the toy rabbit, we were so much alike.

"'It's a very good job,' said Santa, nodding his head at us pleasantly; 'and I shall have to make a lot of these rabbits, for the little children are sure to be greatly pleased with them.'

"So he immediately began to make another, and this time he cut the fur just the right size, so that it was even better than the first rabbit.

"'I must put a squeak in it,' said Santa.

"So he took a box of squeaks from a shelf and put one into the rabbit before he sewed it up. When it was all finished he pressed the toy rabbit with his thumb, and it squeaked so naturally that I jumped off the table, fearing at first the new rabbit was alive. Old Santa laughed merrily at this, and I soon recovered from my fright and was pleased to think the babies were to have such pretty playthings.

"'After this,' said Santa Claus, 'I can make rabbits without having you for a pattern; but if you like you may stay a few days longer in my castle and amuse yourself.'

"I thanked him and decided to stay. So for several days I watched him making all kinds of toys, and I wondered to see how quickly he made them, and how many new things he invented.

"'I almost wish I was a child,' I said to him one day, 'for then I too could have playthings.'

"'Ah, you can run about all day, in summer and in winter, and enjoy yourself in your own way,' said Santa; 'but the poor little children are obliged to stay in the house in the winter and on rainy days in the summer, and then they must have toys to amuse them and keep them contented.'

"I knew this was true, so I only said, admiringly, 'You must be the quickest and the best workman in all the world, Santa.'

"'I suppose I am,' he answered; 'but then, you see, I have been making toys for hundreds of years, and I make so many it is no wonder I am skillful. And now, if you are ready to go home, I'll hitch up the reindeer and take you back again.'

"'Oh, no,' said I, 'I prefer to run by myself, for I can easily find the way and I want to see the country.'

"'If that is the case,' replied Santa, 'I must give you a magic collar to wear, so that you will come to no harm.'

"So, after Mother Hubbard had given me a good meal of turnips and sliced cabbage, Santa Claus put the magic collar around my neck and I started for home. I took my time on the journey, for I knew nothing could harm me, and I saw a good many strange sights before I got back to this place again."

"But what became of the magic collar?" asked Dorothy, who had listened with breathless interest to the rabbit's story.

"After I got home," replied the rabbit, "the collar disappeared from around my neck, and I knew Santa had called it back to himself again. He did not give it to me, you see; he merely let me take it on my journey to protect me. The next Christmas, when I watched by the road-side to see Santa, I was pleased to notice a great many of the toy rabbits sticking out of the loaded sleigh. The babies must have liked them, too, for every year since I have seen them amongst the toys.

"Santa never forgets me, and every time he passes he calls out, in his jolly voice,

"'A merry Christmas to you, Bun Rabbit! The babies still love you dearly.'"

The rabbit paused, and Dorothy was just about to ask another question when Bunny raised his head and seemed to hear something coming.

"What is it?" enquired the girl.

"It's the farmer's big shepherd dog," answered the rabbit, "and I must be going before he sees me, or I shall have to run for my life. So good bye, Dorothy; I hope we shall meet again, and then I will gladly tell you more of my adventures."

The next instant he had sprung into the wood, and all that Dorothy could see of him was a gray streak darting in and out amongst the trees.

THE LIFE AND ADVENTURES OF SANTA CLAUS

ILLUSTRATED BY MARY COWLES CLARK

Original cover for The Life and Adventures of Santa Claus, *1902.*

Original endpaper illustration for The Life and Adventures of Santa Claus, *1902.*

THE LIFE AND ADVENTURES OF
SANTA CLAUS

EDITOR'S NOTE: The Life and Adventures of Santa Claus *was dedicated to Harry Neal Baum, one of L. Frank Baum's four sons, who was 12 years old at the time the book was published.*

To the extent possible, the text of this story, to include spellings such as "wilfully," "good by," and "can not," is left as Baum originally wrote it.

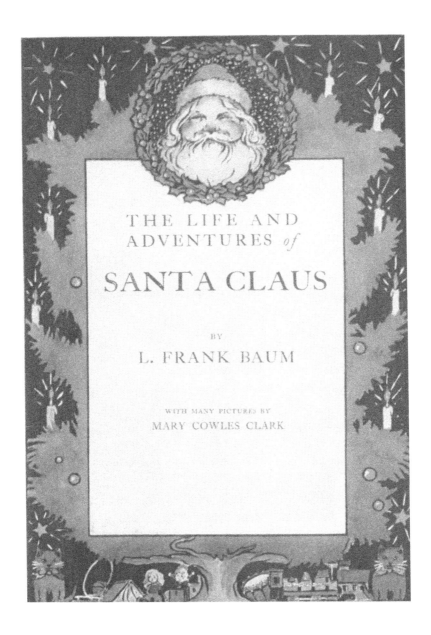

THE LIFE AND ADVENTURES *of*

SANTA CLAUS

BY

L. FRANK BAUM

WITH MANY PICTURES BY

MARY COWLES CLARK

CONTENTS

CHAPTER FIRST

Burzee

HAVE you heard of the great Forest of Burzee? Nurse used to sing of it when I was a child. She sang of the big tree-trunks, standing close together, with their roots intertwining below the earth and their branches intertwining above it; of their rough coating of bark and queer, gnarled limbs; of the bushy foliage that roofed the entire Forest, save where the sunbeams found a path through which to touch the ground in little spots and to cast weird and curious shadows over the mosses, the lichens and the drifts of dried leaves.

The Forest of Burzee is mighty and grand and awesome to those who steal beneath its shade. Coming from the sunlit meadows into its mazes it seems at first gloomy, then pleasant, and afterward filled with never-ending delights.

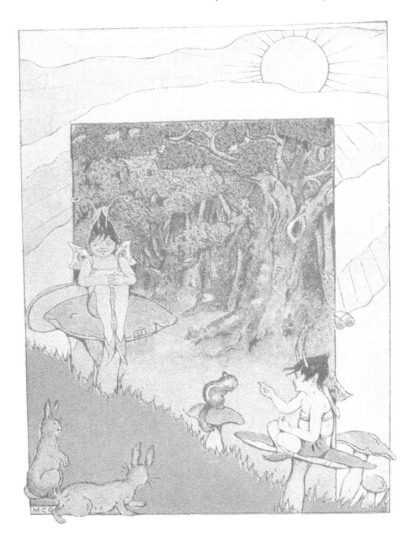

For hundreds of years it has flourished in all its magnificence, the silence of its inclosure unbroken save by the chirp of busy chipmunks, the growl of wild beasts and the songs of birds.

Yet Burzee has its inhabitants—for all this. Nature peopled it in the beginning with Fairies, Knooks, Ryls and Nymphs. As long as the Forest stands it will be a home, a refuge and a playground to these sweet immortals, who revel undisturbed in its depths.

Civilization has never yet reached Burzee. Will it ever, I wonder?

CHAPTER SECOND

The Child of the Forest

ONCE, so long ago our great-grandfathers could scarcely have heard it mentioned, there lived within the great Forest of Burzee a wood-nymph named Necile. She was closely related to the mighty Queen Zurline, and her home was beneath the shade of a wide-spreading oak. Once every year, on Budding Day, when the trees put forth their new buds, Necile held the Golden Chalice of Ak to the lips of the Queen, who drank therefrom to the prosperity of the Forest. So you see she was a nymph of some importance, and, moreover, it is said she was highly regarded because of her beauty and grace.

When she was created she could not have told; Queen Zurline could not have told; the great Ak himself could not have told. It was long ago when the world was new and nymphs were needed to guard the forests and to minister to the wants of the young trees. Then, on some day not remembered, Necile sprang into being; radiant, lovely, straight and slim as the sapling she was created to guard.

Her hair was the color that lines a chestnut-bur; her eyes were blue in the sunlight and purple in the shade; her cheeks bloomed with the faint pink that edges the clouds at sunset; her lips were full red, pouting and sweet. For costume she adopted oak-leaf green; all the wood-nymphs dress in that color and know no other so desirable. Her dainty feet were sandal-clad, while her head remained bare of covering other than her silken tresses.

Necile's duties were few and simple. She kept hurtful weeds from growing beneath her trees and sapping the earth-food required by her charges. She frightened away the Gadgols, who took evil delight in flying against the tree-trunks and wounding them so that they drooped and died from the poisonous contact. In dry seasons she carried water from the brooks and pools and moistened the roots of her thirsty dependents.

That was in the beginning. The weeds had now learned to avoid the forests where wood-nymphs dwelt; the loathsome Gadgols no longer dared come nigh; the trees had become old and sturdy and could bear the drought better than when fresh-sprouted. So Necile's duties were lessened, and time grew laggard, while succeeding years became more tiresome and uneventful than the nymph's joyous spirit loved.

Truly the forest-dwellers did not lack amusement. Each full moon they danced in the Royal Circle of the Queen. There were also the Feast of Nuts, the Jubilee of Autumn Tintings, the solemn ceremony of Leaf Shedding and the revelry of Budding Day. But these periods of enjoyment were far apart, and left many weary hours between.

That a wood-nymph should grow discontented was not thought of by Necile's sisters. It came upon her only after many years of brooding. But when once she had settled in her mind that life was irksome she had no patience with her condition, and longed to do something of real interest and to pass her days in ways hitherto undreamed of by forest nymphs. The Law of the

Forest alone restrained her from going forth in search of adventure.

While this mood lay heavy upon pretty Necile it chanced that the great Ak visited the Forest of Burzee and allowed the wood-nymphs—as was their wont—to lie at his feet and listen to the words of wisdom that fell from his lips. Ak is the Master Woodsman of the world; he sees everything, and knows more than the sons of men.

That night he held the Queen's hand, for he loved the nymphs as a father loves his children; and Necile lay at his feet with many of her sisters and earnestly harkened as he spoke.

"We live so happily, my fair ones, in our forest glades," said Ak, stroking his grizzled beard thoughtfully, "that we know nothing of the sorrow and misery that fall to the lot of those poor mortals who inhabit the open spaces of the earth. They are not of our race, it is true, yet compassion well befits beings so fairly favored as ourselves. Often as I pass by the dwelling of some suffering mortal I am tempted to stop and banish the poor thing's misery. Yet suffering, in moderation, is the natural lot of mortals, and it is not our place to interfere with the laws of Nature."

"Nevertheless," said the fair Queen, nodding her golden head at the Master Woodsman, "it would not be a vain guess that Ak has often assisted these hapless mortals."

Ak smiled.

"Sometimes," he replied, "when they are very young—'children,' the mortals call them—I have stopped to rescue them from misery. The men and women I dare not interfere with; they must bear the burdens Nature has imposed upon them. But the helpless infants, the innocent children of men, have a right to be happy until they become full-grown and able to bear the trials of humanity. So I feel I am justified in assisting them. Not long ago—a year, maybe—I found four poor children huddled in a wooden hut, slowly freezing to death. Their parents had gone to a neighboring village for food, and had left a fire to warm their little ones while they were absent. But a storm arose and drifted the snow in their path, so they were long on the road. Meantime the fire went out and the frost crept into the bones of the waiting children."

"Poor things!" murmured the Queen softly. "What did you do?"

"I called Nelko, bidding him fetch wood from my forests and breathe upon it until the fire blazed again and warmed the little room where the children lay. Then they ceased shivering and fell asleep until their parents came."

"I am glad you did thus," said the good Queen, beaming upon the Master; and Necile, who had eagerly listened to every word, echoed in a whisper: "I, too, am glad!"

"And this very night," continued Ak, "as I came to the edge of Burzee I heard a feeble cry, which I judged came from a human infant. I looked about me and found, close to the Forest, a helpless babe, lying quite naked upon the grasses and wailing piteously. Not far away, screened by the Forest, crouched Shiegra, the lioness, intent upon devouring the infant for her evening meal."

"And what did you do, Ak?" asked the Queen, breathlessly.

"Not much, being in a hurry to greet my nymphs. But I commanded Shiegra to lie close to the babe, and to give it her milk to quiet its hunger. And I told her to send word throughout the Forest, to all beasts and reptiles, that the child should not be harmed."

"I am glad you did thus," said the good Queen again, in a tone of relief; but this time Necile did not echo her words, for the nymph, filled with a strange resolve, had suddenly stolen away from the group.

Swiftly her lithe form darted through the Forest paths until she reached the edge of mighty Burzee, when she paused to gaze curiously about her. Never until now had she ventured so far, for the Law of the Forest had placed the nymphs in its inmost depths.

Necile knew she was breaking the Law, but the thought did not give pause to her dainty feet. She had decided to see with her own eyes this infant Ak had told of, for she had never yet beheld a child of man. All the immortals are full-grown; there are no children among them. Peering through the trees Necile saw the child lying on the grass. But now it was sweetly sleeping, having been comforted by the milk drawn from Shiegra. It was not old enough to know what peril means; if it did not feel hunger it was content.

Softly the nymph stole to the side of the babe and knelt upon the sward, her long robe of rose leaf color spreading about her like a gossamer cloud. Her lovely countenance expressed curiosity and surprise, but, most of all, a tender, womanly pity. The babe was newborn, chubby and pink. It was entirely helpless. While the nymph gazed, the infant opened its eyes, smiled upon her, and stretched out two dimpled arms. In another instant Necile had caught it to her breast and was hurrying with it through the forest paths.

CHAPTER THIRD

The Adoption

THE MASTER WOODSMAN SUDDENLY ROSE, with knitted brows. "There is a strange presence in the Forest," he declared. Then the Queen and her nymphs turned and saw standing before them Necile, with the sleeping infant clasped tightly in her arms and a defiant look in her deep blue eyes.

And thus for a moment they remained, the nymphs filled with surprise and consternation, but the brow of the Master Woodsman gradually clearing as he gazed intently upon the beautiful immortal who had wilfully broken the Law. Then the great Ak, to the wonder of all, laid his hand softly on Necile's flowing locks and kissed her on her fair forehead.

"For the first time within my knowledge," said he, gently, "a nymph has defied me and my laws; yet in my heart can I find no word of chiding. What is your desire, Necile?"

"Let me keep the child!" she answered, beginning to tremble and falling on her knees in supplication.

"Here, in the Forest of Burzee, where the human race has never yet penetrated?" questioned Ak.

"Here, in the Forest of Burzee," replied the nymph, boldly. "It is my home, and I am weary for lack of occupation. Let me care for the babe! See how weak and helpless it is. Surely it can not harm Burzee nor the Master Woodsman of the World!"

"But the Law, child, the Law!" cried Ak, sternly.

"The Law is made by the Master Woodsman," returned Necile; "if he bids me care for the babe he himself has saved from death, who in all the world dare oppose me?" Queen Zurline, who had listened intently to this conversation, clapped her pretty hands gleefully at the nymph's answer.

"You are fairly trapped, O Ak!" she exclaimed, laughing. "Now, I pray you, give heed to Necile's petition."

The Woodsman, as was his habit when in thought, stroked his grizzled beard slowly. Then he said:

"She shall keep the babe, and I will give it my protection. But I warn you all that as this is the first time I have relaxed the Law, so shall it be the last time. Never more, to the end of the World, shall a mortal be adopted by an immortal. Otherwise would we abandon our happy existence for one of trouble and anxiety. Good night, my nymphs!"

Then Ak was gone from their midst, and Necile hurried away to her bower to rejoice over her new-found treasure.

CHAPTER FOURTH

Claus

ANOTHER DAY FOUND Necile's bower the most popular place in the Forest. The nymphs clustered around her and the child that lay asleep in her lap, with expressions of curiosity and delight. Nor were they wanting in praises for the great Ak's kindness in allowing Necile to keep the babe and to care for it. Even the Queen came to peer into the innocent childish face and to hold a helpless, chubby fist in her own fair hand.

"What shall we call him, Necile?" she asked, smiling. "He must have a name, you know."

"Let him be called Claus," answered Necile, "for that means 'a little one.'"

"Rather let him be called Neclaus,"* returned the Queen, "for that will mean 'Necile's little one.'"

[*Some people have spelled this name Nicklaus, and others Nicolas, which is the reason that Santa Claus is still known in some lands as St. Nicolas. But, of course, Neclaus is his right name, and Claus the nickname given him by his adopted mother, the fair nymph Necile.]

The nymphs clapped their hands in delight, and Neclaus became the infant's name, although Necile loved best to call him Claus, and in afterdays many of her sisters followed her example.

Necile gathered the softest moss in all the Forest for Claus to lie upon, and she made his bed in her own bower. Of food the infant had no lack. The nymphs searched the Forest for bell-udders, which grow upon the goa-tree and when opened are found to be filled with sweet milk. And the soft-eyed does willingly gave a share of their milk to support the little stranger, while Shiegra, the lioness, often crept stealthily into Necile's bower and purred softly as she lay beside the babe and fed it.

So the little one flourished and grew big and sturdy day by day, while Necile taught him to speak and to walk and to play.

His thoughts and words were sweet and gentle, for the nymphs knew no evil and their hearts were pure and loving. He became the pet of the Forest, for Ak's decree had forbidden beast or reptile to molest him, and he walked fearlessly wherever his will guided him.

Presently the news reached the other immortals that the nymphs of Burzee had adopted a human infant, and that the act had been sanctioned by the great Ak. Therefore many of them came to visit the little stranger, looking upon him with much interest.

First the Ryls, who are first cousins to the wood-nymphs, although so differently formed. For the Ryls are required to watch over the flowers and plants, as the nymphs watch over the forest trees. They search the wide world for the food required by the roots of the flowering plants, while the brilliant colors possessed by the full-blown flowers are due to the dyes placed in the soil by the Ryls, which are drawn through the little veins in the roots and the body of the plants, as they reach maturity. The Ryls are a busy people, for their flowers bloom and fade continually, but they are merry and light-hearted and are very popular with the other immortals.

 Next came the Knooks, whose duty it is to watch over the beasts of the world, both gentle and wild. The Knooks have a hard time of it, since many of the beasts are ungovernable and rebel against restraint. But they know how to manage them, after all, and you will find that certain laws of the Knooks are obeyed by even the most ferocious animals. Their anxieties make the Knooks look old and worn and crooked, and their natures are a bit rough from associating with wild creatures continually; yet they are most useful to humanity and to the world in general, as their laws are the only laws the forest beasts recognize except those of the Master Woodsman.

Then there were the Fairies, the guardians of mankind, who were much interested in the adoption of Claus because their own laws forbade them to become familiar with their human charges. There are instances on record where the Fairies have shown themselves to human beings, and have even conversed with them; but they are supposed to guard the lives of mankind unseen and unknown, and if they favor some people more than others it is because these have won such distinction fairly, as the Fairies are very just and impartial. But the idea of adopting a child of men had never occurred to them because it was in every way opposed to their laws; so their curiosity was intense to behold the little stranger adopted by Necile and her sister nymphs.

Claus looked upon the immortals who thronged around him with fearless eyes and smiling lips. He rode laughingly upon the shoulders of the merry Ryls; he mischievously pulled the gray beards of the low-browed Knooks; he rested his curly head confidently upon the dainty bosom of the Fairy Queen herself. And the Ryls loved the sound of his laughter; the Knooks loved his courage; the Fairies loved his innocence.

The boy made friends of them all, and learned to know their laws intimately. No Forest flower was trampled beneath his feet, lest the friendly Ryls should be grieved. He never interfered with the beasts of the Forest, lest his friends the Knooks should become angry. The Fairies he loved dearly, but, knowing nothing of mankind, he could not understand that he was the only one of his race admitted to friendly intercourse with them.

Indeed, Claus came to consider that he alone, of all the Forest people, had no like nor fellow. To him the Forest was the world. He had no idea that millions of toiling, striving human creatures existed.

And he was happy and content.

CHAPTER FIFTH

The Master Woodsman

YEARS PASS SWIFTLY IN BURZEE, for the nymphs have no need to regard time in any way. Even centuries make no change in the dainty creatures; ever and ever they remain the same, immortal and unchanging.

Claus, however, being mortal, grew to manhood day by day. Necile was disturbed, presently, to find him too big to lie in her lap, and he had a desire for other food than milk. His stout legs carried him far into Burzee's heart, where he gathered supplies of nuts and berries, as well as several sweet and wholesome roots, which suited his stomach better than the bell-udders. He sought Necile's bower less frequently, till finally it became his custom to return thither only to sleep.

The nymph, who had come to love him dearly, was puzzled to comprehend the changed nature of her charge, and unconsciously altered her own mode of life to conform to his whims. She followed him readily through the forest paths, as did many of her sister nymphs, explaining as they walked all the mysteries of the gigantic wood and the habits and nature of the living things which dwelt beneath its shade.

The language of the beasts became clear to little Claus; but he never could understand their sulky and morose tempers. Only the squirrels, the mice and the rabbits seemed to possess cheerful and merry natures; yet would the boy laugh when the panther growled, and stroke the bear's glossy coat while the creature snarled and bared its teeth menacingly. The growls and snarls were not for Claus, he well knew, so what did they matter?

He could sing the songs of the bees, recite the poetry of the wood-flowers and relate the history of every blinking owl in Burzee. He helped the Ryls to feed their plants and the Knooks to keep order among the animals. The little immortals regarded him as a privileged person, being especially protected by Queen Zurline and her nymphs and favored by the great Ak himself.

One day the Master Woodsman came back to the Forest of Burzee. He had visited, in turn, all his forests throughout the world, and they were many and broad.

Not until he entered the glade where the Queen and her nymphs were assembled to greet him did Ak remember the child he had permitted Necile to adopt. Then he found, sitting familiarly in the circle of lovely immortals, a broad-shouldered, stalwart youth, who, when erect, stood fully as high as the shoulder of the Master himself.

Ak paused, silent and frowning, to bend his piercing gaze upon Claus. The clear eyes met his own steadfastly, and the Woodsman gave a sigh of relief as he marked their placid depths and read the youth's brave and innocent heart. Nevertheless, as Ak sat beside the fair Queen, and the golden chalice, filled with rare nectar, passed from lip to lip, the Master Woodsman was strangely silent and reserved, and stroked his beard many times with a thoughtful motion.

With morning he called Claus aside, in kindly fashion, saying:

"Bid good by, for a time, to Necile and her sisters; for you shall accompany me on my journey through the world."

The venture pleased Claus, who knew well the honor of being companion of the Master Woodsman of the world. But Necile wept for the first time in her life, and clung to the boy's neck as if she could not bear to let him go. The nymph who had mothered this sturdy youth was still as dainty, as charming and beautiful as when she had dared to face Ak with the babe clasped to her breast; nor was her love less great. Ak beheld the two clinging together, seemingly as brother and sister to one another, and again he wore his thoughtful look.

CHAPTER SIXTH

Claus Discovers Humanity

TAKING Claus to a small clearing in the Forest, the Master said: "Place your hand upon my girdle and hold fast while we journey through the air; for now shall we encircle the world and look upon many of the haunts of those men from whom you are descended."

These words caused Claus to marvel, for until now he had thought himself the only one of his kind upon the earth; yet in silence he grasped firmly the girdle of the great Ak, his astonishment forbidding speech.

Then the vast Forest of Burzee seemed to fall away from their feet, and the youth found himself passing swiftly through the air at a great height.

Ere long there were spires beneath them, while buildings of many shapes and colors met their downward view. It was a city of men, and Ak, pausing to descend, led Claus to its inclosure. Said the Master:

"So long as you hold fast to my girdle you will remain unseen by all mankind, though seeing clearly yourself. To release your grasp will be to separate yourself forever from me and your home in Burzee."

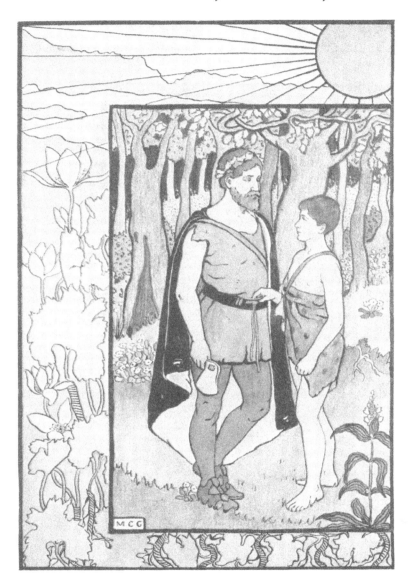

One of the first laws of the Forest is obedience, and Claus had no thought of disobeying the Master's wish. He clung fast to the girdle and remained invisible.

Thereafter with each moment passed in the city the youth's

wonder grew. He, who had supposed himself created differently from all others, now found the earth swarming with creatures of his own kind.

"Indeed," said Ak, "the immortals are few; but the mortals are many."

Claus looked earnestly upon his fellows. There were sad faces, gay and reckless faces, pleasant faces, anxious faces and kindly faces, all mingled in puzzling disorder. Some worked at tedious tasks; some strutted in impudent conceit; some were thoughtful and grave while others seemed happy and content. Men of many natures were there, as everywhere, and Claus found much to please him and much to make him sad.

But especially he noted the children—first curiously, then eagerly, then lovingly. Ragged little ones rolled in the dust of the streets, playing with scraps and pebbles. Other children, gaily dressed, were propped upon cushions and fed with sugar-plums. Yet the children of the rich were not happier than those playing with the dust and pebbles, it seemed to Claus.

"Childhood is the time of man's greatest content," said Ak, following the youth's thoughts. "'Tis during these years of innocent pleasure that the little ones are most free from care."

"Tell me," said Claus, "why do not all these babies fare alike?"

"Because they are born in both cottage and palace," returned the Master. "The difference in the wealth of the parents determines the lot of the child. Some are carefully tended and clothed in silks and dainty linen; others are neglected and covered with rags."

"Yet all seem equally fair and sweet," said Claus, thoughtfully.

"While they are babes—yes;" agreed Ak. "Their joy is in being alive, and they do not stop to think. In after years the doom of mankind overtakes them, and they find they must struggle and worry, work and fret, to gain the wealth that is so dear to the hearts of men. Such things are unknown in the Forest where you were reared." Claus was silent a moment. Then he asked:

"Why was I reared in the Forest, among those who are not of my race?"

Then Ak, in gentle voice, told him the story of his babyhood: how he had been abandoned at the Forest's edge and left a prey to wild beasts, and how the loving nymph Necile had rescued him and brought him to manhood under the protection of the immortals.

"Yet I am not of them," said Claus, musingly.

"You are not of them," returned the Woodsman. "The nymph who cared for you as a mother seems now like a sister to you; by and by, when you grow old and gray, she will seem like a daughter. Yet another brief span and you will be but a memory, while she remains Necile."

"Then why, if man must perish, is he born?" demanded the boy.

"Everything perishes except the world itself and its keepers," answered Ak. "But while life lasts everything on earth has its use. The wise seek ways to be helpful to the world, for the helpful ones are sure to live again."

Much of this Claus failed to understand fully, but a longing seized him to become helpful to his fellows, and he remained grave and thoughtful while they resumed their journey.

They visited many dwellings of men in many parts of the world, watching farmers toil in the fields, warriors dash into cruel fray, and merchants exchange their goods for bits of white and yellow metal. And everywhere the eyes of Claus sought out the children in love and pity, for the thought of his own helpless babyhood was strong within him and he yearned to give help to the innocent little ones of his race even as he had been succored by the kindly nymph.

Day by day the Master Woodsman and his pupil traversed the earth, Ak speaking but seldom to the youth who clung steadfastly to his girdle, but guiding him into all places where he might become familiar with the lives of human beings.

And at last they returned to the grand old Forest of Burzee, where the Master set Claus down within the circle of nymphs, among whom the pretty Necile anxiously awaited him.

The brow of the great Ak was now calm and peaceful; but the brow of Claus had become lined with deep thought. Necile sighed at the change in her foster-son, who until now had been ever joyous and smiling, and the thought came to her that never again would the life of the boy be the same as before this eventful journey with the Master.

CHAPTER SEVENTH

Claus Leaves the Forest

WHEN GOOD QUEEN ZURLINE had touched the golden chalice with her fair lips and it had passed around the circle in honor of the travelers' return, the Master Woodsman of the World, who had not yet spoken, turned his gaze frankly upon Claus and said:

"Well?"

The boy understood, and rose slowly to his feet beside Necile. Once only his eyes passed around the familiar circle of nymphs, every one of whom he remem-

bered as a loving comrade; but tears came unbidden to dim his sight, so he gazed thereafter steadfastly at the Master.

"I have been ignorant," said he, simply, "until the great Ak in his kindness taught me who and what I am. You, who live so sweetly in your forest bowers, ever fair and youthful and innocent, are no fit comrades for a son of humanity. For I have looked upon man, finding him doomed to live for a brief space upon earth, to toil for the things he needs, to fade into old age, and then to pass away as the leaves in autumn. Yet every man has his mission, which is to leave the world better, in some way, than he found it. I am of the race of men, and man's lot is my lot. For your tender care of the poor, forsaken babe you adopted, as well as for your loving comradeship during my boyhood, my heart will ever overflow with gratitude. My foster-mother," here he stopped and kissed Necile's white forehead, "I shall love and cherish while life lasts. But I must leave you, to take my part in the endless struggle to which humanity is doomed, and to live my life in my own way."

"What will you do?" asked the Queen, gravely.

"I must devote myself to the care of the children of mankind, and try to make them happy," he answered. "Since your own tender care of a babe brought to me happiness and strength, it is just and right that I devote my life to the pleasure of other babes. Thus will the memory of the loving nymph Necile be planted within the hearts of thousands of my race for many years to come, and her kindly act be recounted in song and in story while the world shall last. Have I spoken well, O Master?"

"You have spoken well," returned Ak, and rising to his feet he continued: "Yet one thing must not be forgotten. Having been adopted as the child of the Forest, and the playfellow of the nymphs, you have gained a distinction which forever separates you from your kind. Therefore, when you go forth into the world of men you shall retain the protection of the Forest, and the powers you now enjoy will remain with you to assist you in your labors. In any need you may call upon the Nymphs, the Ryls, the Knooks and the Fairies, and they will serve you gladly. I, the Master Woodsman of the World, have said it, and my Word is the Law!"

Claus looked upon Ak with grateful eyes.

"This will make me mighty among men," he replied. "Protected by these kind friends I may be able to make thousands of little children happy. I will try very hard to do my duty, and I know the Forest people will give me their sympathy and help."

"We will!" said the Fairy Queen, earnestly.

"We will!" cried the merry Ryls, laughing.

"We will!" shouted the crooked Knooks, scowling.

"We will!" exclaimed the sweet nymphs, proudly. But Necile said nothing. She only folded Claus in her arms and kissed him tenderly.

"The world is big," continued the boy, turning again to his loyal friends, "but men are everywhere. I shall begin my work near my friends, so that if I meet with misfortune I can come to the Forest for counsel or help."

With that he gave them all a loving look and turned away. There was no need to say good by, but for him the sweet, wild life of the Forest was over. He went forth bravely to meet his doom—the doom of the race of man—the necessity to worry and work.

But Ak, who knew the boy's heart, was merciful and guided his steps.

COMING through Burzee to its eastern edge Claus reached the Laughing Valley of Hohaho. On each side were rolling green hills, and a brook wandered midway between them to wind afar off beyond the valley. At his back was the grim Forest; at the far end of the valley a broad plain. The eyes of the young man, which had until now reflected his grave thoughts, became brighter as he stood silent, looking out upon the Laughing Valley. Then on a sudden his eyes twinkled, as stars do on a still night, and grew merry and wide.

For at his feet the cowslips and daisies smiled on him in friendly regard; the breeze whistled gaily as it passed by and fluttered the locks on his forehead; the brook laughed joyously as it leaped over the pebbles and swept around the green curves of its banks; the bees sang sweet songs as they flew from dandelion to daffodil; the beetles chirruped happily in the long grass, and the sunbeams glinted pleasantly over all the scene.

"Here," cried Claus, stretching out his arms as if to embrace the Valley, "will I make my home!"

That was many, many years ago. It has been his home ever since. It is his home now.

MANHOOD

CHAPTER FIRST

The Laughing Valley

WHEN CLAUS CAME the Valley was empty save for the grass, the brook, the wildflowers, the bees and the butterflies. If he would make his home here and live after the fashion of men he must have a house. This puzzled him at first, but while he stood smiling in the sunshine, he suddenly found beside him old Nelko, the servant of the Master Woodsman. Nelko bore an ax, strong and broad, with a blade that gleamed like burnished silver. This he placed in the young man's hand, then disappeared without a word.

Claus understood, and turning to the Forest's edge he selected a number of fallen tree-trunks, which he began to clear of their

dead branches. He would not cut into a living tree. His life among the nymphs who guarded the Forest had taught him that a live tree is sacred, being a created thing endowed with feeling. But with the dead and fallen trees it was different. They had fulfilled their destiny, as active members of the Forest community, and now it was fitting that their remains should minister to the needs of man.

The ax bit deep into the logs at every stroke. It seemed to have a force of its own, and Claus had but to swing and guide it.

When shadows began creeping over the green hills to lie in the Valley overnight, the young man had chopped many logs into equal lengths and proper shapes for building a house such as he had seen the poorer classes of men inhabit. Then, resolving to await another day before he tried to fit the logs together, Claus ate some of the sweet roots he well knew how to find, drank deeply from the laughing brook, and lay down to sleep on the grass, first seeking a spot where no flowers grew, lest the weight of his body should crush them.

And while he slumbered and breathed in the perfume of the wondrous Valley the Spirit of Happiness crept into his heart and drove out all terror and care and misgivings. Never more would the face of Claus be clouded with anxieties; never more would the trials of life weigh him down as with a burden. The Laughing Valley had claimed him for its own.

Would that we all might live in that delightful place!—but then, maybe, it would become overcrowded. For ages it had awaited a tenant. Was it chance that led young Claus to make his home in this happy vale? Or may we guess that his thoughtful friends, the immortals, had directed his steps when he wandered away from Burzee to seek a home in the great world?

Certain it is that while the moon peered over the hilltop and flooded with its soft beams the body of the sleeping stranger, the Laughing Valley was filled with the queer, crooked shapes of the friendly Knooks. These people spoke no words, but worked with skill and swiftness. The logs Claus had trimmed with his bright ax were carried to a spot beside the brook and fitted one upon another, and during the night a strong and roomy dwelling was built.

The birds came sweeping into the Valley at daybreak, and their songs, so seldom heard in the deep wood, aroused the stranger. He rubbed the web of sleep from his eyelids and looked around. The house met his gaze.

"I must thank the Knooks for this," said he, gratefully. Then he walked to his dwelling and entered at the doorway. A large room faced him, having a fireplace at the end

and a table and bench in the middle. Beside the fireplace was a cupboard. Another doorway was beyond. Claus entered here, also, and saw a smaller room with a bed against the wall and a stool set near a small stand. On the bed were many layers of dried moss brought from the Forest.

"Indeed, it is a palace!" exclaimed the smiling Claus. "I must thank the good Knooks again, for their knowledge of man's needs as well as for their labors in my behalf."

He left his new home with a glad feeling that he was not quite alone in the world, although he had chosen to abandon his Forest life. Friendships are not easily broken, and the immortals are everywhere.

Upon reaching the brook he drank of the pure water, and then sat down on the bank to laugh at the mischievous gambols of the ripples as they pushed one another against rocks or crowded desperately to see which should first reach the turn beyond. And as they raced away he listened to the song they sang:

> *"Rushing, pushing, on we go!*
> *Not a wave may gently flow—*
> *All are too excited.*
> *Ev'ry drop, delighted,*
> *Turns to spray in merry play*
> *As we tumble on our way!"*

Next Claus searched for roots to eat, while the daffodils turned their little eyes up to him laughingly and lisped their dainty song:

> *"Blooming fairly, growing rarely,*
> *Never flowerets were so gay!*
> *Perfume breathing, joy bequeathing,*
> *As our colors we display."*

It made Claus laugh to hear the little things voice their happiness as they nodded gracefully on their stems. But another strain caught his ear as the sunbeams fell gently across his face and whispered:

> *"Here is gladness, that our rays*
> *Warm the valley through the days;*
> *Here is happiness, to give*
> *Comfort unto all who live!"*

"Yes!" cried Claus in answer, "there is happiness and joy in all things here. The Laughing Valley is a valley of peace and good-will."

He passed the day talking with the ants and beetles and exchanging jokes with the light-hearted butterflies. And at night he lay on his bed of soft moss and slept soundly.

Then came the Fairies, merry but noiseless, bringing skillets and pots and dishes and pans and all the tools necessary to prepare food and to comfort a mortal. With these they filled cupboard and fireplace, finally placing a stout suit of wool clothing on the stool by the bedside.

When Claus awoke he rubbed his eyes again, and laughed, and spoke aloud his thanks to the Fairies and the Master Woodsman who had sent them. With eager joy he examined all his new possessions, wondering what some might be used for. But, in the days when he had clung to the girdle of the great Ak and visited the cities of men, his eyes had been quick to note all the manners and customs of the race to which he belonged; so he guessed from the gifts brought by the Fairies that the Master expected him hereafter to live in the fashion of his fellow-creatures.

"Which means that I must plow the earth and plant corn," he reflected; "so that when winter comes I shall have garnered food in plenty."

But, as he stood in the grassy Valley, he saw that to turn up the earth in furrows would be to destroy hundreds of pretty, helpless flowers, as well as thousands of the tender blades of grass. And this he could not bear to do.

Therefore he stretched out his arms and uttered a peculiar whistle he had learned in the Forest, afterward crying:

"Ryls of the Field Flowers—come to me!"

Instantly a dozen of the queer little Ryls were squatting upon the ground before him, and they nodded to him in cheerful greeting.

Claus gazed upon them earnestly.

"Your brothers of the Forest," he said, "I have known and loved many years. I shall love you, also,

when we have become friends. To me the laws of the Ryls, whether those of the Forest or of the field, are sacred. I have never wilfully destroyed one of the flowers you tend so carefully; but I must plant grain to use for food during the cold winter, and how am I to do this without killing the little creatures that sing to me so prettily of their fragrant blossoms?"

The Yellow Ryl, he who tends the buttercups, made answer:

"Fret not, friend Claus. The great Ak has spoken to us of you. There is better work for you in life than to labor for food, and though, not being of the Forest, Ak has no command over us, nevertheless are we glad to favor one he loves. Live, therefore, to do the good work you are resolved to undertake. We, the Field Ryls, will attend to your food supplies."

After this speech the Ryls were no longer to be seen, and Claus drove from his mind the thought of tilling the earth.

When next he wandered back to his dwelling a bowl of fresh milk stood upon the table; bread was in the cupboard and sweet honey filled a dish beside it. A pretty basket of rosy apples and new-plucked grapes was also awaiting him. He called out "Thanks, my friends!" to the invisible Ryls, and straightway began to eat of the food.

Thereafter, when hungry, he had but to look into the cupboard to find goodly supplies brought by the kindly Ryls. And the Knooks cut and stacked much wood for his fireplace. And the Fairies brought him warm blankets and clothing.

So began his life in the Laughing Valley, with the favor and friendship of the immortals to minister to his every want.

CHAPTER SECOND

How Claus Made the First Toy

TRULY OUR CLAUS HAD WISDOM, for his good fortune but strengthened his resolve to befriend the little ones of his own race. He knew his plan was approved by the immortals, else they would not have favored him so greatly.

So he began at once to make acquaintance with mankind. He walked through the Valley to the plain beyond, and crossed the plain in many directions to reach the abodes of men. These stood singly or in groups of dwellings called villages, and in nearly all the houses, whether big or little, Claus found children.

The youngsters soon came to know his merry, laughing face and the kind glance of his bright eyes; and the parents, while they regarded the young man with some scorn for loving children more than their elders, were content that the girls and boys had found a playfellow who seemed willing to amuse them.

So the children romped and played games with Claus, and the boys rode upon his shoulders, and the girls nestled in his strong arms, and the babies clung fondly to his knees. Wherever the young man chanced to be, the sound of childish laughter followed him; and to understand this better you must know that children were much neglected in those days and received little attention from their parents, so that it became to them a marvel that so goodly a man as Claus devoted his time to making them happy. And those who knew him were, you may be sure, very happy indeed. The sad faces of the poor and abused grew bright for once; the cripple smiled despite his misfortune; the ailing ones hushed their moans and the grieved ones their cries when their merry friend came nigh to comfort them.

Only at the beautiful palace of the Lord of Lerd and at the frowning castle of the Baron Braun was Claus refused admittance. There were children at both places; but the servants at the palace shut the door in the young stranger's face, and the fierce Baron threatened to hang him from an iron hook on the castle walls. Whereupon Claus sighed and went back to the poorer dwellings where he was welcome.

After a time the winter drew near.

The flowers lived out their lives and faded and disappeared; the beetles burrowed far into the warm earth; the butterflies deserted the meadows; and the voice of the brook grew hoarse, as if it had taken cold.

One day snowflakes filled all the air in the Laughing Valley, dancing boisterously toward the earth and clothing in pure white raiment the roof of Claus's dwelling.

At night Jack Frost rapped at the door.

"Come in!" cried Claus.

"Come out!" answered Jack, "for you have a fire inside."

So Claus came out. He had known Jack Frost in the Forest, and liked the jolly rogue, even while he mistrusted him.

"There will be rare sport for me to-night, Claus!" shouted the sprite. "Isn't this glorious weather? I shall nip scores of noses and ears and toes before daybreak."

"If you love me, Jack, spare the children," begged Claus.

"And why?" asked the other, in surprise.

"They are tender and helpless," answered Claus.

"But I love to nip the tender ones!" declared Jack. "The older ones are tough, and tire my fingers."

"The young ones are weak, and can not fight you," said Claus.

"True," agreed Jack, thoughtfully. "Well, I will not pinch a child this night—if I can resist the temptation," he promised. "Good night, Claus!"

"Good night."

The young man went in and closed the door, and Jack Frost ran on to the nearest village.

Claus threw a log on the fire, which burned up brightly. Beside the hearth sat Blinkie, a big cat given him by Peter the Knook. Her fur was soft and glossy, and she purred never-ending songs of contentment.

"I shall not see the children again soon," said Claus to the cat, who kindly paused in her song to listen. "The winter is upon us, the snow will be deep for many days, and I shall be unable to play with my little friends."

The cat raised a paw and stroked her nose thoughtfully, but made no reply. So long as the fire burned and Claus sat in his easy chair by the hearth she did not mind the weather.

So passed many days and many long evenings. The cupboard was always full, but Claus became weary with having nothing to do more than to feed the fire from the big wood-pile the Knooks had brought him.

One evening he picked up a stick of wood and began to cut it with his sharp knife. He had no thought, at first, except to occupy his time, and he whistled and sang to the cat as he carved away portions of the stick. Puss sat up on her haunches and watched him, listening at the same time to her master's merry whistle, which she loved to hear even more than her own purring songs.

Claus glanced at puss and then at the stick he was whit-tling, until presently the wood began to have a shape, and the shape was like the head of a cat, with two ears sticking upward.

Claus stopped whistling to laugh, and then both he and the cat looked at the wooden image in some surprise. Then he carved out the eyes and the nose, and rounded the lower part of the head so that it rested upon a neck.

Puss hardly knew what to make of it now, and sat up stiffly, as if watching with some suspicion what would come next.

Claus knew. The head gave him an idea. He plied his knife carefully and with skill, forming slowly the body of the cat, which he made to sit upon its haunches as the real cat did, with her tail wound around her two front legs.

The work cost him much time, but the evening was long and he had nothing better to do. Finally he gave a loud and delighted laugh at the result of his labors and placed the wooden cat, now completed, upon the hearth opposite the real one.

Puss thereupon glared at her image, raised her hair in anger, and uttered a defiant mew. The wooden cat paid no attention, and Claus, much amused, laughed again.

Then Blinkie advanced toward the wooden image to eye it closely and smell of it intelligently. Eyes and nose told her the creature was wood, in spite of its natural appearance; so puss resumed her seat and her purring, but as she neatly washed her face with her padded paw she cast more than one admiring glance at her clever master. Perhaps she felt the same satisfaction we feel when we look upon good photographs of ourselves.

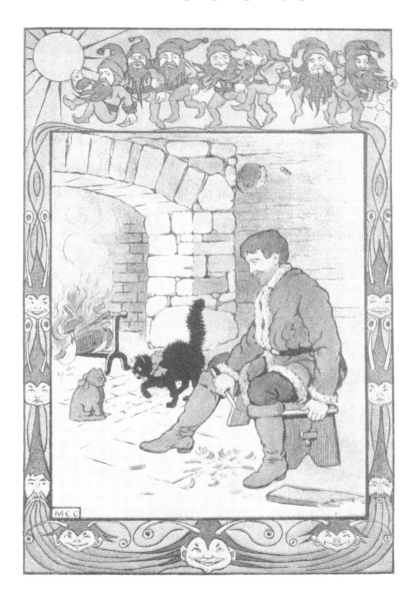

The cat's master was himself pleased with his handiwork, without knowing exactly why. Indeed, he had great cause to congratulate himself that night, and all the children throughout the world should have joined him rejoicing. For Claus had made his first toy.

CHAPTER THIRD

How the Ryls Colored the Toys

A HUSH LAY on the Laughing Valley now. Snow covered it like a white spread and pillows of downy flakes drifted before the dwelling where Claus sat feeding the blaze of the fire. The brook gurgled on beneath a heavy sheet of ice and all living plants and insects nestled close to Mother Earth to keep warm. The face of the moon was hid by dark clouds, and the wind, delighting in the wintry sport, pushed and whirled the snowflakes in so many directions that they could get no chance to fall to the ground.

Claus heard the wind whistling and shrieking in its play and thanked the good Knooks again for his comfortable shelter. Blinkie washed her face lazily and stared at the coals with a look of perfect content. The toy cat sat opposite the real one and gazed straight ahead, as toy cats should.

Suddenly Claus heard a noise that sounded different from the voice of the wind. It was more like a wail of suffering and despair.

He stood up and listened, but the wind, growing boisterous, shook the door and rattled the windows to distract his attention. He waited until the wind was tired and then, still listening, he heard once more the shrill cry of distress.

Quickly he drew on his coat, pulled his cap over his eyes and opened the door. The wind dashed in and scattered the embers over the hearth, at the same time blowing Blinkie's fur so furiously that she crept under the table to escape. Then the door was closed and Claus was outside, peering anxiously into the darkness.

The wind laughed and scolded and tried to push him over, but he stood firm. The helpless flakes stumbled against his eyes and dimmed his sight, but he rubbed them away and looked again. Snow was everywhere, white and glittering. It covered the earth and filled the air.

The cry was not repeated.

Claus turned to go back into the house, but the wind caught him unawares and he stumbled and fell across a snowdrift. His hand plunged into the drift and touched something that was not snow. This he seized and, pulling it gently toward him, found it to be a child. The next moment he had lifted it in his arms and carried it into the house.

The wind followed him through the door, but Claus shut it out quickly. He laid the rescued child on the hearth, and brushing away the snow he discovered it to be Weekum, a little boy who lived in a house beyond the Valley.

Claus wrapped a warm blanket around the little one and rubbed the frost from its limbs. Before long the child opened his eyes and, seeing where he was, smiled happily. Then Claus warmed milk and fed it to the boy slowly, while the cat looked on with sober curiosity. Finally the little one curled up in his friend's arms and sighed and fell asleep, and Claus, filled with gladness that he had found the wanderer, held him closely while he slumbered.

The wind, finding no more mischief to do, climbed the hill and swept on toward the north. This gave the weary snowflakes time to settle down to earth, and the Valley became still again.

The boy, having slept well in the arms of his friend, opened his eyes and sat up. Then, as a child will, he looked around the room and saw all that it contained.

"Your cat is a nice cat, Claus," he said, at last. "Let me hold it."

But puss objected and ran away.

"The other cat won't run, Claus," continued the boy. "Let me hold that one." Claus placed the toy in his arms, and the boy held it lovingly and kissed the tip of its wooden ear.

"How did you get lost in the storm, Weekum?" asked Claus.

"I started to walk to my auntie's house and lost my way," answered Weekum.

"Were you frightened?"

"It was cold," said Weekum, "and the snow got in my eyes, so I could not see. Then I kept on till I fell in the snow, without knowing where I was, and the wind blew the flakes over me and covered me up."

Claus gently stroked his head, and the boy looked up at him and smiled.

"I'm all right now," said Weekum.

"Yes," replied Claus, happily. "Now I will put you in my warm bed, and you must sleep until morning, when I will carry you back to your mother."

"May the cat sleep with me?" asked the boy.

"Yes, if you wish it to," answered Claus.

"It's a nice cat!" Weekum said, smiling, as Claus tucked the blankets around him; and presently the little one fell asleep with the wooden toy in his arms.

When morning came the sun claimed the Laughing Valley and flooded it with his rays; so Claus prepared to take the lost child back to its mother.

"May I keep the cat, Claus?" asked Weekum. "It's nicer than real cats. It doesn't run away, or scratch or bite. May I keep it?"

"Yes, indeed," answered Claus, pleased that the toy he had made could give pleasure to the child. So he wrapped the boy and the wooden cat in a warm cloak, perching the bundle upon his own broad shoulders, and then he tramped through the snow and the drifts of the Valley and across the plain beyond to the poor cottage where Weekum's mother lived.

"See, mama!" cried the boy, as soon as they entered, "I've got a cat!"

The good woman wept tears of joy over the rescue of her darling and thanked Claus many times for his kind act. So he carried a warm and happy heart back to his home in the Valley.

That night he said to puss: "I believe the children will love the wooden cats almost as well as the real ones, and they can't hurt them by pulling their tails and ears. I'll make another."

So this was the beginning of his great work.

 The next cat was better made than the first. While Claus sat whittling it out the Yellow Ryl came in to make him a visit, and so pleased was he with the man's skill that he ran away and brought several of his fellows.

There sat the Red Ryl, the Black Ryl, the Green Ryl, the Blue Ryl and the Yellow Ryl in a circle on the floor, while Claus whittled and whistled and the wooden cat grew into shape.

"If it could be made the same color as the real cat, no one would know the difference," said the Yellow Ryl, thoughtfully.

"The little ones, maybe, would not know the difference," replied Claus, pleased with the idea.

"I will bring you some of the red that I color my roses and tulips with," cried the Red Ryl; "and then you can make the cat's lips and tongue red."

"I will bring some of the green that I color my grasses and leaves with," said the Green Ryl; "and then you can color the cat's eyes green."

"They will need a bit of yellow, also," remarked the Yellow Ryl; "I must fetch some of the yellow that I use to color my buttercups and goldenrods with."

"The real cat is black," said the Black Ryl; "I will bring some of the black that I use to color the eyes of my pansies with, and then you can paint your wooden cat black."

"I see you have a blue ribbon around Blinkie's neck," added the Blue Ryl. "I will get some of the color that I use to paint the bluebells and forget-me-nots with, and then you can carve a wooden ribbon on the toy cat's neck and paint it blue."

So the Ryls disappeared, and by the time Claus had finished carving out the form of the cat they were all back with the paints and brushes.

They made Blinkie sit upon the table, that Claus might paint the toy cat just the right color, and when the work was done the Ryls declared it was exactly as good as a live cat.

"That is, to all appearances," added the Red Ryl.

Blinkie seemed a little offended by the attention bestowed upon the toy, and that she might not seem to approve the imitation cat she walked to the corner of the hearth and sat down with a dignified air.

But Claus was delighted, and as soon as morning came he

started out and tramped through the snow, across the Valley and the plain, until he came to a village. There, in a poor hut near the walls of the beautiful palace of the Lord of Lerd, a little girl lay upon a wretched cot, moaning with pain.

Claus approached the child and kissed her and comforted her, and then he drew the toy cat from beneath his coat, where he had hidden it, and placed it in her arms.

Ah, how well he felt himself repaid for his labor and his long walk when he saw the little one's eyes grow bright with pleasure! She hugged the kitty tight to her breast, as if it had been a precious gem, and would not let it go for a single moment. The fever was quieted, the pain grew less, and she fell into a sweet and refreshing sleep.

Claus laughed and whistled and sang all the way home. Never had he been so happy as on that day.

When he entered his house he found Shiegra, the lioness, awaiting him. Since his babyhood Shiegra had loved Claus, and while he dwelt in the Forest she had often come to visit him at Necile's bower. After Claus had gone to live in the Laughing Valley Shiegra became lonely and ill at ease, and now she had braved the snow-drifts, which all lions abhor, to see him once more. Shiegra was getting old and her teeth were beginning to fall out, while the hairs that tipped her ears and tail had changed from tawny-yellow to white.

Claus found her lying on his hearth, and he put his arms around the neck of the lioness and hugged her lovingly. The cat had retired into a far corner. She did not care to associate with Shiegra.

Claus told his old friend about the cats he had made, and how much pleasure they had given Weekum and the sick girl. Shiegra did not know much about chil- dren; indeed, if she met a child she could scarcely be trusted not to devour it. But she was interested in Claus' new labors, and said:

"These images seem to me very attractive. Yet I can not see why you should make cats, which are very unimportant animals. Suppose, now that I am here, you make the image of a lioness, the Queen of all beasts. Then, indeed, your children will be happy—and safe at the same time!"

Claus thought this was a good suggestion. So he got a piece of wood and sharpened his knife, while Shiegra crouched upon the hearth at his feet. With much care he carved the head in the likeness of the lioness, even to the two fierce teeth that curved over her lower lip and the deep, frowning lines above her wide-open eyes.

When it was finished he said:

"You have a terrible look, Shiegra."

"Then the image is like me," she answered; "for I am indeed terrible to all who are not my friends."

Claus now carved out the body, with Shiegra's long tail trailing behind it. The image of the crouching lioness was very life-like.

"It pleases me," said Shiegra, yawning and stretching her body gracefully. "Now I will watch while you paint."

He brought the paints the Ryls had given him from the cupboard and colored the image to resemble the real Shiegra.

The lioness placed her big, padded paws upon the edge of

the table and raised herself while she carefully examined the toy that was her likeness.

"You are indeed skillful!" she said, proudly. "The children will like that better than cats, I'm sure."

Then snarling at Blinkie, who arched her back in terror and whined fearfully, she walked away toward her forest home with stately strides.

CHAPTER FOURTH

How Little Mayrie Became Frightened

THE WINTER WAS OVER NOW, and all the Laughing Valley was filled with joyous excitement. The brook was so happy at being free once again that it gurgled more boisterously than ever and dashed so recklessly against the rocks that it sent showers of spray high in the air. The grass thrust its sharp little blades upward through the mat of dead stalks where it had hidden from the snow, but the flowers were yet too timid to show themselves, although the Ryls were busy feeding their roots. The sun was in remarkably good humor, and sent his rays dancing merrily throughout the Valley.

Claus was eating his dinner one day when he heard a timid knock on his door.

"Come in!" he called.

No one entered, but after a pause came another rapping.

Claus jumped up and threw open the door. Before him stood a small girl holding a smaller brother fast by the hand.

"Is you Tlaus?" she asked, shyly.

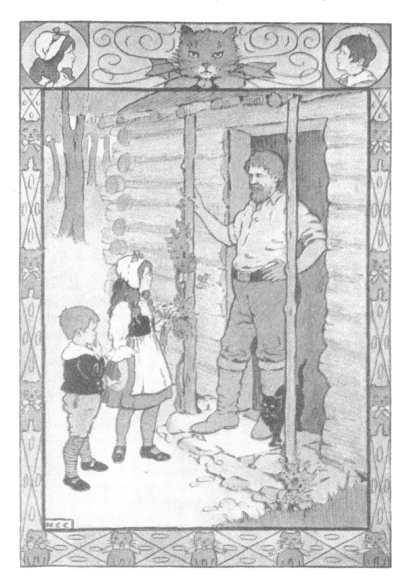

"Indeed I am, my dear!" he answered, with a laugh, as he caught both children in his arms and kissed them. "You are very welcome, and you have come just in time to share my dinner."

He took them to the table and fed them with fresh milk and nut-cakes.

When they had eaten enough he asked:

"Why have you made this long journey to see me?"

"I wants a tat!" replied little Mayrie; and her brother, who had not yet learned to speak many words, nodded his head and exclaimed like an echo: "Tat!"

"Oh, you want my toy cats, do you?" returned Claus, greatly pleased to discover that his creations were so popular with children.

The little visitors nodded eagerly.

"Unfortunately," he continued, "I have but one cat now ready, for I carried two to children in the town yesterday. And the one I have shall be given to your brother, Mayrie, because he is the smaller; and the next one I make shall be for you."

The boy's face was bright with smiles as he took the precious toy Claus held out to him; but little Mayrie covered her face with her arm and began to sob grievously.

"I—I—I wants a t—t—tat now!" she wailed.

Her disappointment made Claus feel miserable for a moment. Then he suddenly remembered Shiegra.

"Don't cry, darling!" he said, soothingly; "I have a toy much nicer than a cat, and you shall have that."

He went to the cupboard and drew out the image of the lioness, which he placed on the table before Mayrie.

The girl raised her arm and gave one glance at the fierce teeth and glaring eyes of the beast, and then, uttering a terrified scream, she rushed from the house. The boy followed her, also screaming lustily, and even dropping his precious cat in his fear.

For a moment Claus stood motionless, being puzzled and astonished. Then he threw Shiegra's image into the cupboard and ran after the children, calling to them not to be frightened.

Little Mayrie stopped in her flight and her brother clung to her skirt; but they both cast fearful glances at the house until Claus had assured them many times that the beast had been locked in the cupboard.

"Yet why were you frightened at seeing it?" he asked. "It is only a toy to play with!"

"It's bad!" said Mayrie, decidedly, "an'—an'—just horrid, an' not a bit nice, like tats!"

"Perhaps you are right," returned Claus, thoughtfully. "But if you will return with me to the house I will soon make you a pretty cat."

So they timidly entered the house again, having faith in their friend's words; and afterward they had the joy of watching Claus carve out a cat from a bit of wood and paint it in natural colors. It did not take him long to do this, for he had become skillful with his knife by this time, and Mayrie loved her toy the more dearly because she had seen it made.

After his little visitors had trotted away on their journey homeward Claus sat long in deep thought. And he then decided that such fierce creatures as his friend the lioness would never do as models from which to fashion his toys.

"There must be nothing to frighten the dear babies," he reflected; "and while I know Shiegra well, and am not afraid of her, it is but natural that children should look upon her image with terror. Hereafter I will choose such mild-mannered animals as squirrels and rabbits and deer and lambkins from which to carve my toys, for then the little ones will love rather than fear them."

He began his work that very day, and before bedtime had made a wooden rabbit and a lamb. They were not quite so life-like as the cats had been, because they were formed from memory, while Blinkie had sat very still for Claus to look at while he worked.

But the new toys pleased the children nevertheless, and the fame of Claus' playthings quickly spread to every cottage on plain and in village. He always carried his gifts to the sick or crippled children, but those who were strong enough walked to the house in the Valley to ask for them, so a little path was soon worn from the plain to the door of the toy-maker's cottage.

First came the children who had been playmates of Claus, before he began to make toys. These, you may be sure, were well supplied. Then children who lived farther away heard of the wonderful images and made journeys to the Valley to secure them. All little ones were welcome, and never a one went away empty-handed.

This demand for his handiwork kept Claus busily occupied, but he was quite happy in knowing the pleasure he gave to so many of the dear children. His friends the immortals were pleased with his success and supported him bravely.

The Knooks selected for him clear pieces of soft wood, that his knife might not be blunted in cutting them; the Ryls kept him supplied with paints of all colors and brushes fashioned from the tips of timothy grasses; the Fairies discovered that the workman needed saws and chisels and hammers and nails, as well as knives, and brought him a goodly array of such tools.

Claus soon turned his living room into a most wonderful workshop. He built a bench before the window, and arranged his tools and paints so that he could reach everything as he sat on his stool. And as he finished toy after toy to delight the hearts of little children he found himself growing so gay and happy that he could not refrain from singing and laughing and whistling all the day long.

"It's because I live in the Laughing Valley, where everything else laughs!" said Claus.

But that was not the reason.

CHAPTER FIFTH

How Bessie Blithesome Came to the Laughing Valley

ONE DAY, as Claus sat before his door to enjoy the sunshine while he busily carved the head and horns of a toy deer, he looked up and discovered a glittering cavalcade of horsemen approaching through the Valley.

When they drew nearer he saw that the band consisted of a score of men-at-arms, clad in bright armor and bearing in their hands spears and battle-axes. In front of these rode little Bessie Blithesome, the pretty daughter of that proud Lord of Lerd who had once driven Claus from his palace. Her palfrey was pure white, its bridle was covered with glittering gems, and its saddle draped with cloth of gold, richly broidered. The soldiers were sent to protect her from harm while she journeyed.

Claus was surprised, but he continued to whittle and to sing until the cavalcade drew up before him. Then the little girl leaned over the neck of her palfrey and said:

"Please, Mr. Claus, I want a toy!"

Her voice was so pleading that Claus jumped up at once and stood beside her. But he was puzzled how to answer her request.

"You are a rich lord's daughter," said he, "and have all that you desire."

"Except toys," added Bessie. "There are no toys in all the world but yours."

"And I make them for the poor children, who have nothing else to amuse them," continued Claus.

"Do poor children love to play with toys more than rich ones?" asked Bessie.

"I suppose not," said Claus, thoughtfully.

"Am I to blame because my father is a lord? Must I be denied the pretty toys I long for because other children are poorer than I?" she inquired earnestly.

"I'm afraid you must, dear," he answered; "for the poor have nothing else with which to amuse themselves. You have your pony to ride, your servants to wait on you, and every comfort that money can procure."

"But I want toys!" cried Bessie, wiping away the tears that forced themselves into her eyes. "If I can not have them, I shall be very unhappy."

Claus was troubled, for her grief recalled to him the thought that his desire was to make all children happy, without regard to their condition in life. Yet, while so many poor children were clamoring for his toys he could not bear to give one of them to Bessie Blithesome, who had so much already to make her happy.

"Listen, my child," said he, gently; "all the toys I am now making are promised to others. But the next shall be yours, since your heart so longs for it. Come to me again in two days and it shall be ready for you."

Bessie gave a cry of delight, and leaning over her pony's neck she kissed Claus prettily upon his forehead. Then, calling to her men-at-arms, she rode gaily away, leaving Claus to resume his work.

"If I am to supply the rich children as well as the poor ones," he thought, "I shall not have a spare moment in the whole year! But is it right I should give to the rich? Surely I must go to Necile and talk with her about this matter."

So when he had finished the toy deer, which was very like a deer he had known in the Forest glades, he walked into Burzee and made his way to the bower of the beautiful Nymph Necile, who had been his foster mother.

She greeted him tenderly and lovingly, listening with interest to his story of the visit of Bessie Blithesome.

"And now tell me," said he, "shall I give toys to rich children?"

"We of the Forest know nothing of riches," she replied. "It seems to me that one child is like another child, since they are all made of the same clay, and that riches are like a gown, which may be put on or taken away, leaving the child unchanged. But the Fairies are guardians of mankind, and know mortal children better than I. Let us call the Fairy Queen."

This was done, and the Queen of the Fairies sat beside them and heard Claus relate his reasons for thinking the rich children could get along without his toys, and also what the Nymph had said.

"Necile is right," declared the Queen; "for, whether it be rich or poor, a child's longings for pretty playthings are but natural. Rich Bessie's heart may suffer as much grief as poor Mayrie's; she can be just as lonely and discontented, and just as gay and happy. I think, friend Claus, it is your duty to make all little ones glad, whether they chance to live in palaces or in cottages."

"Your words are wise, fair Queen," replied Claus, "and my heart tells me they are as just as they are wise. Hereafter all children may claim my services."

Then he bowed before the gracious Fairy and, kissing Necile's red lips, went back into his Valley.

At the brook he stopped to drink, and afterward he sat on the bank and took a piece of moist clay in his hands while he thought what sort of toy he should make for Bessie Blithesome. He did not notice that his fingers were working the clay into shape until, glancing downward, he found he had unconsciously formed a head that bore a slight resemblance to the Nymph Necile!

At once he became interested. Gathering more of the clay from the bank he carried it to his house. Then, with the aid of his knife and a bit of wood he succeeded in working the clay into the image of a toy nymph. With skillful strokes he formed long, waving hair on the head and covered the body with a gown of oakleaves, while the two feet sticking out at the bottom of the gown were clad in sandals.

But the clay was soft, and Claus found he must handle it gently to avoid ruining his pretty work.

"Perhaps the rays of the sun will draw out the moisture and cause the clay to become hard," he thought. So he laid the image on a flat board and placed it in the glare of the sun.

This done, he went to his bench and began painting the toy deer, and soon he became so interested in the work that he forgot all about the clay nymph. But next morning, happening to notice it as it lay on the board, he found the sun had baked it to the hardness of stone, and it was strong enough to be safely handled.

Claus now painted the nymph with great care in the likeness of Necile, giving it deep-blue eyes, white teeth, rosy lips and ruddy-brown hair. The gown he colored oak-leaf green, and when the paint was dry Claus himself was charmed with the new toy. Of course it was not nearly so lovely as the real Necile; but, considering the material of which it was made, Claus thought it was very beautiful.

When Bessie, riding upon her white palfrey, came to his dwelling next day, Claus presented her with the new toy. The little girl's eyes were brighter than ever as she examined the pretty image, and she loved it at once, and held it close to her breast, as a mother does to her child.

"What is it called, Claus?" she asked.

Now Claus knew that Nymphs do not like to be spoken of by mortals, so he could not tell Bessie it was an image of Necile he had given her. But as it was a new toy he searched his mind for a new name to call it by, and the first word he thought of he decided would do very well.

"It is called a dolly, my dear," he said to Bessie.

"I shall call the dolly my baby," returned Bessie, kissing it fondly; "and I shall tend it and care for it just as Nurse cares for me. Thank you very much, Claus; your gift has made me happier than I have ever been before!"

Then she rode away, hugging the toy in her arms, and Claus, seeing her delight, thought he would make another dolly, better and more natural than the first.

He brought more clay from the brook, and remembering that Bessie had called the dolly her baby he resolved to form this one into a baby's image. That was no difficult task to the clever workman, and soon the baby dolly was lying on the board and placed in the sun to dry. Then, with the clay that was left, he began to make an image of Bessie Blithesome herself.

This was not so easy, for he found he could not make the silken robe of the lord's daughter out of the common clay. So he called the Fairies to his aid, and asked them to bring him colored silks with which to make a real dress for the clay image. The Fairies set off at once on their errand, and before nightfall they returned with a generous supply of silks and laces and golden threads.

Claus now became impatient to complete his new dolly, and instead of waiting for the next day's sun he placed the clay image upon his hearth and covered it over with glowing coals. By morning, when he drew the dolly from the ashes, it had baked as hard as if it had lain a full day in the hot sun.

Now our Claus became a dressmaker as well as a toymaker. He cut the lavender silk, and neatly sewed it into a beautiful gown that just fitted the new dolly. And he put a lace collar around its neck and pink silk shoes on its feet. The natural color of baked clay is a light gray, but Claus painted the face to resemble the color of flesh, and he gave the dolly Bessie's brown eyes and golden hair and rosy cheeks.

It was really a beautiful thing to look upon, and sure to bring joy to some childish heart. While Claus was admiring it he heard a knock at his door, and little Mayrie entered. Her face was sad and her eyes red with continued weeping.

"Why, what has grieved you, my dear?" asked Claus, taking the child in his arms.

"I've—I've—bwoke my tat!" sobbed Mayrie.

"How?" he inquired, his eyes twinkling.

"I—I dwopped him, an' bwoke off him's tail; an'—an'—then I dwopped him an' bwoke off him's ear! An'—an' now him's all spoilt!"

Claus laughed.

"Never mind, Mayrie dear," he said. "How would you like this new dolly, instead of a cat?"

Mayrie looked at the silk-robed dolly and her eyes grew big with astonishment.

"Oh, Tlaus!" she cried, clapping her small hands together with rapture; "tan I have 'at boo'ful lady?"

"Do you like it?" he asked.

"I love it!" said she. "It's better 'an tats!"

"Then take it, dear, and be careful not to break it."

Mayrie took the dolly with a joy that was almost reverent, and her face dimpled with smiles as she started along the path toward home.

6. THE WICKEDNESS OF THE AWGWAS

CHAPTER SIXTH

The Wickedness of the Awgwas

I MUST NOW TELL you something about the Awgwas, that terrible race of creatures which caused our good Claus so much trouble and nearly succeeded in robbing the children of the world of their earliest and best friend.

I do not like to mention the Awgwas, but they are a part of this history, and can not be ignored. They were neither mortals nor immortals, but stood midway between those classes of beings. The Awgwas were invisible to ordinary people, but not to immortals. They could pass swiftly through the air from one part of the world to another, and had the power of influencing the minds of human beings to do their wicked will.

They were of gigantic stature and had coarse, scowling countenances which showed plainly their hatred of all mankind. They possessed no consciences whatever and delighted only in evil deeds.

Their homes were in rocky, mountainous places, from whence they sallied forth to accomplish their wicked purposes.

The one of their number that could think of the most horrible deed for them to do was always elected the King Awgwa, and all the race obeyed his orders. Sometimes these creatures lived to become a hundred years old, but usually they fought so fiercely among themselves that many were destroyed in combat, and when they died that was the end of them. Mortals were powerless to harm them and the immortals shuddered when the Awgwas were mentioned, and always avoided them. So they flourished for many years unopposed and accomplished much evil.

I am glad to assure you that these vile creatures have long since perished and passed from Earth; but in the days when Claus was making his first toys they were a numerous and powerful tribe.

One of the principal sports of the Awgwas was to inspire angry passions in the hearts of little children, so that they quarreled and fought with one another. They would tempt boys to eat of unripe fruit, and then delight in the pain they suffered; they urged little girls to disobey their parents, and then would laugh when the children were punished. I do not know what causes a child to be naughty in these days, but when the Awgwas were on earth naughty children were usually under their influence.

Now, when Claus began to make children happy he kept them out of the power of the Awgwas; for children possessing such lovely playthings as he gave them had no wish to obey the evil thoughts the Awgwas tried to thrust into their minds.

Therefore, one year when the wicked tribe was to elect a new King, they chose an Awgwa who proposed to destroy Claus and take him away from the children.

"There are, as you know, fewer naughty children in the world since Claus came to the Laughing Valley and began to make his toys," said the new King, as he squatted upon a rock and looked around at the scowling faces of his people. "Why, Bessie Blithesome has not stamped her foot once this month, nor has Mayrie's brother slapped his sister's face or thrown the puppy into the rain-barrel. Little Weekum took his bath last night without screaming or struggling, because his mother had promised he should take his toy cat to bed with him! Such a condition of affairs is awful for any Awgwa to think of, and the only way we can direct the naughty actions of children is to take this person Claus away from them."

"Good! good!" cried the big Awgwas, in a chorus, and they clapped their hands to applaud the speech of the King.

"But what shall we do with him?" asked one of the creatures.

"I have a plan," replied the wicked King; and what his plan was you will soon discover.

That night Claus went to bed feeling very happy, for he had completed no less than four pretty toys during the day, and they were sure, he thought, to make four little children happy. But while he slept the band of invisible Awgwas surrounded his bed, bound him with stout cords, and then flew away with him to the middle of a dark forest in far off Ethop, where they laid him down and left him.

When morning came Claus found himself thousands of miles from any human being, a prisoner in the wild jungle of an unknown land.

From the limb of a tree above his head swayed a huge python, one of those reptiles that are able to crush a man's bones in their coils. A few yards away crouched a savage panther, its glaring red eyes fixed full on the helpless Claus. One of those monstrous spotted spiders whose sting is death crept stealthily toward him over the matted leaves, which shriveled and turned black at its very touch.

But Claus had been reared in Burzee, and was not afraid.

"Come to me, ye Knooks of the Forest!" he cried, and gave the low, peculiar whistle that the Knooks know.

The panther, which was about to spring upon its victim, turned and slunk away. The python swung itself into the tree and disappeared among the leaves. The spider stopped short in its advance and hid beneath a rotting log.

Claus had no time to notice them, for he was surrounded by a band of harsh-featured Knooks, more crooked and deformed in appearance than any he had ever seen.

"Who are you that call on us?" demanded one, in a gruff voice.

"The friend of your brothers in Burzee," answered Claus. "I

have been brought here by my enemies, the Awgwas, and left to perish miserably. Yet now I implore your help to release me and to send me home again."

"Have you the sign?" asked another.

"Yes," said Claus.

They cut his bonds, and with his free arms he made the secret sign of the Knooks.

Instantly they assisted him to stand upon his feet, and they brought him food and drink to strengthen him.

"Our brothers of Burzee make queer friends," grumbled an ancient Knook whose flowing beard was pure white. "But he who knows our secret sign and signal is entitled to our help, whoever he may be. Close your eyes, stranger, and we will conduct you to your home. Where shall we seek it?"

"'Tis in the Laughing Valley," answered Claus, shutting his eyes.

"There is but one Laughing Valley in the known world, so we can not go astray," remarked the Knook.

As he spoke the sound of his voice seemed to die away, so Claus opened his eyes to see what caused the change. To his astonishment he found himself seated on the bench by his own door, with the Laughing Valley spread out before him. That day he visited the Wood-Nymphs and related his adventure to Queen Zurline and Necile.

"The Awgwas have become your enemies," said the lovely Queen, thoughtfully; "so we must do all we can to protect you from their power."

"It was cowardly to bind him while he slept," remarked Necile, with indignation.

"The evil ones are ever cowardly," answered Zurline, "but our friend's slumber shall not be disturbed again."

The Queen herself came to the dwelling of Claus that evening and placed her Seal on every door and window, to keep out the Awgwas. And under the Seal of Queen Zurline was placed the Seal of the Fairies and the Seal of the Ryls and the Seal of the Knooks, that the charm might become more powerful.

And Claus carried his toys to the children again, and made many more of the little ones happy.

You may guess how angry the King Awgwa and his fierce band were when it was known to them that Claus had escaped from the Forest of Ethop.

They raged madly for a whole week, and then held another meeting among the rocks.

"It is useless to carry him where the Knooks reign," said the King, "for he has their protection. So let us cast him into a cave of our own mountains, where he will surely perish."

This was promptly agreed to, and the wicked band set out that night to seize Claus. But they found his dwelling guarded by the Seals of the Immortals and were obliged to go away baffled and disappointed.

"Never mind," said the King; "he does not sleep always!"

Next day, as Claus traveled to the village across the plain, where he intended to present a toy squirrel to a lame boy, he was suddenly set upon by the Awgwas, who seized him and carried him away to the mountains.

There they thrust him within a deep cavern and rolled many huge rocks against the entrance to prevent his escape.

Deprived thus of light and food, and with little air to breathe, our Claus was, indeed, in a pitiful plight. But he spoke the mystic words of the Fairies, which always command their friendly aid, and they came to his rescue and transported him to the Laughing Valley in the twinkling of an eye.

Thus the Awgwas discovered they might not destroy one

who had earned the friendship of the immortals; so the evil band sought other means of keeping Claus from bringing happiness to children and so making them obedient.

Whenever Claus set out to carry his toys to the little ones, an Awgwa, who had been set to watch his movements, sprang upon him and snatched the toys from his grasp. And the children were no more disappointed than was Claus when he was obliged to return home disconsolate. Still he persevered, and made many toys for his little friends and started with them for the villages. And always the Awgwas robbed him as soon as he had left the Valley.

They threw the stolen playthings into one of their lonely caverns, and quite a heap of toys accumulated before Claus became discouraged and gave up all attempts to leave the Valley. Then children began coming to him, since they found he did not go to them; but the wicked Awgwas flew around them and caused their steps to stray and the paths to become crooked, so never a little one could find a way into the Laughing Valley.

Lonely days now fell upon Claus, for he was denied the pleasure of bringing happiness to the children whom he had learned to love. Yet he bore up bravely, for he thought surely the time would come when the Awgwas would abandon their evil designs to injure him.

He devoted all his hours to toy-making, and when one plaything had been completed he stood it on a shelf he had built for that purpose. When the shelf became filled with rows of toys he made another one, and filled that also. So that in time he had many shelves filled with gay and beautiful toys representing horses, dogs, cats, elephants, lambs, rabbits and deer, as well as pretty dolls of all sizes and balls and marbles of baked clay painted in gay colors.

Often, as he glanced at this array of childish treasures, the heart of good old Claus became sad, so greatly did he long to carry the toys to his children. And at last, because he could bear it no longer, he ventured to go to the great Ak, to whom he told the story of his persecution by the Awgwas, and begged the Master Woodsman to assist him.

CHAPTER SEVENTH

The Great Battle Between Good and Evil

AK LISTENED GRAVELY to the recital of Claus, stroking his beard the while with the slow, graceful motion that betokened deep thought. He nodded approvingly when Claus told how the Knooks and Fairies had saved him from death, and frowned when he heard how the Awgwas had stolen the children's toys. At last he said:

"From the beginning I have approved the work you are doing among the children of men, and it annoys me that your good deeds should be thwarted by the Awgwas. We immortals have no connection whatever with the evil creatures who have attacked you. Always have we avoided them, and they, in turn, have hitherto taken care not to cross our pathway. But in this matter I find they have interfered with one of our friends, and I will ask them to abandon their persecutions, as you are under our protection."

Claus thanked the Master Woodsman most gratefully and returned to his Valley, while Ak, who never delayed carrying out his promises, at once traveled to the mountains of the Awgwas.

There, standing on the bare rocks, he called on the King and his people to appear.

Instantly the place was filled with throngs of the scowling Awgwas, and their King, perching himself on a point of rock, demanded fiercely:

"Who dares call on us?"

"It is I, the Master Woodsman of the World," responded Ak.

"Here are no forests for you to claim," cried the King, angrily. "We owe no allegiance to you, nor to any immortal!"

"That is true," replied Ak, calmly. "Yet you have ventured to interfere with the actions of Claus, who dwells in the Laughing Valley, and is under our protection."

Many of the Awgwas began muttering at this speech, and their King turned threateningly on the Master Woodsman.

"You are set to rule the forests, but the plains and the valleys are ours!" he shouted. "Keep to your own dark woods! We will do as we please with Claus."

"You shall not harm our friend in any way!" replied Ak.

"Shall we not?" asked the King, impudently. "You will see! Our powers are vastly superior to those of mortals, and fully as great as those of immortals."

"It is your conceit that misleads you!" said Ak, sternly. "You are a transient race, passing from life into nothingness. We, who live forever, pity but despise you. On Earth you are scorned by all, and in Heaven you have no place! Even the mortals, after their earth life, enter another existence for all time, and so are your superiors. How then dare you, who are neither mortal nor immortal, refuse to obey my wish?"

The Awgwas sprang to their feet with menacing gestures, but their King motioned them back.

"Never before," he cried to Ak, while his voice trembled with rage, "has an immortal declared himself the master of the

Awgwas! Never shall an immortal venture to interfere with our actions again! For we will avenge your scornful words by killing your friend Claus within three days. Nor you, nor all the immortals can save him from our wrath. We defy your powers! Begone, Master Woodsman of the World! In the country of the Awgwas you have no place."

"It is war!" declared Ak, with flashing eyes.

"It is war!" returned the King, savagely. "In three days your friend will be dead."

The Master turned away and came to his Forest of Burzee, where he called a meeting of the immortals and told them of the defiance of the Awgwas and their purpose to kill Claus within three days.

The little folk listened to him quietly.

"What shall we do?" asked Ak.

"These creatures are of no benefit to the world," said the Prince of the Knooks; "we must destroy them."

"Their lives are devoted only to evil deeds," said the Prince of the Ryls. "We must destroy them."

"They have no conscience, and endeavor to make all mortals as bad as themselves," said the Queen of the Fairies. "We must destroy them."

"They have defied the great Ak, and threaten the life of our adopted son," said beautiful Queen Zurline. "We must destroy them."

The Master Woodsman smiled.

"You speak well," said he. "These Awgwas we know to be a

powerful race, and they will fight desperately; yet the outcome is certain. For we who live can never die, even though conquered by our enemies, while every Awgwa who is struck down is one foe the less to oppose us. Prepare, then, for battle, and let us resolve to show no mercy to the wicked!"

Thus arose that terrible war between the immortals and the spirits of evil which is sung of in Fairyland to this very day.

The King Awgwa and his band determined to carry out the threat to destroy Claus. They now hated him for two reasons: he made children happy and was a friend of the Master Woodsman. But since Ak's visit they had reason to fear the opposition of the immortals, and they dreaded defeat. So the King sent swift messengers to all parts of the world to summon every evil creature to his aid.

And on the third day after the declaration of war a mighty army was at the command of the King Awgwa. There were three hundred Asiatic Dragons, breathing fire that consumed everything it touched. These hated mankind and all good spirits. And there were the three-eyed Giants of Tatary, a host in themselves, who liked nothing better than to fight. And next came the Black Demons from Patalonia, with great spreading wings like those of a bat, which swept terror and misery through the world as they beat upon the air. And joined to these were the Goozzle-Goblins, with long talons as sharp as swords, with which they clawed the flesh from their foes. Finally, every mountain Awgwa in the world had come to participate in the great battle with the immortals.

The King Awgwa looked around upon this vast army and his heart beat high with wicked pride, for he believed he would surely triumph over his gentle enemies, who had never before been known to fight. But the Master Woodsman had not been idle. None of his people was used to warfare, yet now that they were called upon to face the hosts of evil they willingly prepared for the fray.

Ak had commanded them to assemble in the Laughing Valley, where Claus, ignorant of the terrible battle that was to be waged on his account, was quietly making his toys.

Soon the entire Valley, from hill to hill, was filled with the little immortals. The Master Woodsman stood first, bearing a gleaming ax that shone like burnished silver. Next came the Ryls, armed with sharp thorns from bramble-bushes. Then the Knooks, bearing the spears they used when they were forced to prod their savage beasts into submission. The Fairies, dressed in white gauze with rainbow-hued wings, bore golden wands, and the Wood-Nymphs, in their uniforms of oak-leaf green, carried switches from ash trees as weapons.

Loud laughed the Awgwa King when he beheld the size and the arms of his foes. To be sure the mighty ax of the Woodsman was to be dreaded, but the sweet-faced Nymphs and pretty Fairies, the gentle Ryls and crooked Knooks were such harmless folk that he almost felt shame at having called such a terrible host to oppose them.

"Since these fools dare fight," he said to the leader of the Tatary Giants, "I will overwhelm them with our evil powers!"

To begin the battle he poised a great stone in his left hand and cast it full against the sturdy form of the Master Woodsman, who turned it aside with his ax. Then rushed the three-eyed Giants of Tatary upon the Knooks, and the Goozzle-Goblins upon the Ryls, and the fire-breathing Dragons upon the sweet Fairies. Because the Nymphs were Ak's own people the band of Awgwas sought them out, thinking to overcome them with ease.

But it is the Law that while Evil, unopposed, may accomplish terrible deeds, the powers of Good can never be overthrown when opposed to Evil. Well had it been for the King Awgwa had he known the Law!

His ignorance cost him his existence, for one flash of the ax borne by the Master Woodsman of the World cleft the wicked King in twain and rid the earth of the vilest creature it contained.

Greatly marveled the Tatary Giants when the spears of the little Knooks pierced their thick walls of flesh and sent them reeling to the ground with howls of agony.

Woe came upon the sharp-taloned Goblins when the thorns of the Ryls reached their savage hearts and let their life-blood sprinkle all the plain. And afterward from every drop a thistle grew.

The Dragons paused astonished before the Fairy wands, from whence rushed a power that caused their fiery breaths to flow back on themselves so that they shriveled away and died.

As for the Awgwas, they had scant time to realize how they were destroyed, for the ash switches of the Nymphs bore a charm unknown to any Awgwa, and turned their foes into clods of earth at the slightest touch!

When Ak leaned upon his gleaming ax and turned to look over the field of battle he saw the few Giants who were able to run disappearing over the distant hills on their return to Tatary. The Goblins had perished every one, as had the terrible Dragons, while all that remained of the wicked Awgwas was a great number of earthen hillocks dotting the plain.

And now the immortals melted from the Valley like dew at sunrise, to resume their duties in the Forest, while Ak walked slowly and thoughtfully to the house of Claus and entered.

"You have many toys ready for the children," said the

Woodsman, "and now you may carry them across the plain to the dwellings and the villages without fear."

"Will not the Awgwas harm me?" asked Claus, eagerly.

"The Awgwas," said Ak, "have perished!"

NOW I WILL GLADLY HAVE DONE with wicked spirits and with fighting and bloodshed. It was not from choice that I told of the Awgwas and their allies, and of their great battle with the immortals. They were part of this history, and could not be avoided.

CHAPTER EIGHTH

The First Journey with the Reindeer

THOSE WERE happy days for Claus when he carried his accumulation of toys to the children who had awaited them so long. During his imprisonment in the Valley he had been so industrious that all his shelves were filled with playthings, and after quickly supplying the little ones living near by he saw he must now extend his travels to wider fields.

Remembering the time when he had journeyed with Ak through all the world, he knew children were everywhere, and he longed to make as many as possible happy with his gifts.

So he loaded a great sack with all kinds of toys, slung it upon his back that he might carry it more easily, and started off on a longer trip than he had yet undertaken.

Wherever he showed his merry face, in hamlet or in farmhouse, he received a cordial welcome, for his fame had spread into far lands. At each village the children swarmed about him, following his footsteps wherever he went; and the women thanked him gratefully for the joy he brought their little ones; and the men looked upon him curiously that he should devote his time to such a queer occupation as toy-making. But every one smiled on him and gave him kindly words, and Claus felt amply repaid for his long journey.

When the sack was empty he went back again to the Laughing Valley and once more filled it to the brim. This time he followed another road, into a different part of the country, and carried happiness to many children who never before had owned a toy or guessed that such a delightful plaything existed.

After a third journey, so far away that Claus was many days walking the distance, the store of toys became exhausted and without delay he set about making a fresh supply.

From seeing so many children and studying their tastes he had acquired several new ideas about toys.

The dollies were, he had found, the most delightful of all playthings for babies and little girls, and often those who could not say "dolly" would call for a "doll" in their sweet baby talk. So Claus resolved to make many dolls, of all sizes, and to dress them in bright-colored clothing. The older boys—and even some of the girls—loved the images of animals, so he still made cats and elephants and horses. And many of the little fellows had musical natures, and longed for drums and cymbals and whistles and horns. So he made a number of toy drums, with tiny sticks to beat them with; and he made whistles from the willow trees, and horns from the bog-reeds, and cymbals from bits of beaten metal.

All this kept him busily at work, and before he realized it the winter season came, with deeper snows than usual, and he knew he could not leave the Valley with his heavy pack. Moreover, the next trip would take him farther from home than ever before, and Jack Frost was mischievous enough to nip his nose and ears if he undertook the long journey while the Frost King reigned. The Frost King was Jack's father and never reproved him for his pranks.

So Claus remained at his work-bench; but he whistled and sang as merrily as ever, for he would allow no disappointment to sour his temper or make him unhappy.

One bright morning he looked from his window and saw

two of the deer he had known in the Forest walking toward his house.

Claus was surprised; not that the friendly deer should visit him, but that they walked on the surface of the snow as easily as if it were solid ground, notwithstanding the fact that throughout the Valley the snow lay many feet deep. He had walked out of his house a day or two before and had sunk to his armpits in a drift.

So when the deer came near he opened the door and called to them:

"Good morning, Flossie! Tell me how you are able to walk on the snow so easily."

"It is frozen hard," answered Flossie.

"The Frost King has breathed on it," said Glossie, coming up, "and the surface is now as solid as ice."

"Perhaps," remarked Claus, thoughtfully, "I might now carry my pack of toys to the children."

"Is it a long journey?" asked Flossie.

"Yes; it will take me many days, for the pack is heavy," answered Claus.

"Then the snow would melt before you could get back," said the deer. "You must wait until spring, Claus."

Claus sighed. "Had I your fleet feet," said he, "I could make the journey in a day."

"But you have not," returned Glossie, looking at his own slender legs with pride.

"Perhaps I could ride upon your back," Claus ventured to remark, after a pause.

"Oh no; our backs are not strong enough to bear your weight," said Flossie, decidedly. "But if you had a sledge, and could harness us to it, we might draw you easily, and your pack as well."

"I'll make a sledge!" exclaimed Claus. "Will you agree to draw me if I do?"

"Well," replied Flossie, "we must first go and ask the Knooks, who are our guardians, for permission; but if they consent, and you can make a sledge and harness, we will gladly assist you."

"Then go at once!" cried Claus, eagerly. "I am sure the friendly Knooks will give their consent, and by the time you are back I shall be ready to harness you to my sledge."

Flossie and Glossie, being deer of much intelligence, had long wished to see the great world, so they gladly ran over the frozen snow to ask the Knooks if they might carry Claus on his journey.

Meantime the toy-maker hurriedly began the construction of a sledge, using material from his wood-pile. He made two long runners that turned upward at the front ends, and across these nailed short boards, to make a platform. It was soon completed, but was as rude in appearance as it is possible for a sledge to be.

The harness was more difficult to prepare, but Claus twisted strong cords together and knotted them so they would fit around the necks of the deer, in the shape of a collar. From these ran other cords to fasten the deer to the front of the sledge.

Before the work was completed Glossie and Flossie were back from the Forest, having been granted permission by Will Knook to make the journey with Claus provided they would return to Burzee by daybreak the next morning.

"That is not a very long time," said Flossie; "but we are swift and strong, and if we get started by this evening we can travel many miles during the night."

Claus decided to make the attempt, so he hurried on his

preparations as fast as possible. After a time he fastened the collars around the necks of his steeds and harnessed them to his rude sledge. Then he placed a stool on the little platform, to serve as a seat, and filled a sack with his prettiest toys.

"How do you intend to guide us?" asked Glossie. "We have never been out of the Forest before, except to visit your house, so we shall not know the way."

Claus thought about that for a moment. Then he brought more cords and fastened two of them to the spreading antlers of each deer, one on the right and the other on the left.

"Those will be my reins," said Claus, "and when I pull them to the right or to the left you must go in that direction. If I do not pull the reins at all you may go straight ahead."

"Very well," answered Glossie and Flossie; and then they asked: "Are you ready?"

Claus seated himself upon the stool, placed the sack of toys at his feet, and then gathered up the reins.

"All ready!" he shouted; "away we go!"

The deer leaned forward, lifted their slender limbs, and the next moment away flew the sledge over the frozen snow. The swiftness of the motion surprised Claus, for in a few strides they were across the Valley and gliding over the broad plain beyond.

The day had melted into evening by the time they started; for, swiftly as Claus had worked, many hours had been consumed in making his preparations. But the moon shone brightly to light their way, and Claus soon decided it was just as pleasant to travel by night as by day.

The deer liked it better; for, although they wished to see something of the world, they were timid about meeting men, and now all the dwellers in the towns and farmhouses were sound asleep and could not see them.

Away and away they sped, on and on over the hills and through the valleys and across the plains until they reached a village where Claus had never been before.

Here he called on them to stop, and they immediately

obeyed. But a new difficulty now presented itself, for the people had locked their doors when they went to bed, and Claus found he could not enter the houses to leave his toys.

"I am afraid, my friends, we have made our journey for nothing," said he, "for I shall be obliged to carry my playthings back home again without giving them to the children of this village."

"What's the matter?" asked Flossie.

"The doors are locked," answered Claus, "and I can not get in."

Glossie looked around at the houses. The snow was quite deep in that village, and just before them was a roof only a few feet above the sledge. A broad chimney, which seemed to Glossie big enough to admit Claus, was at the peak of the roof.

"Why don't you climb down that chimney?" asked Glossie.

Claus looked at it.

"That would be easy enough if I were on top of the roof," he answered.

"Then hold fast and we will take you there," said the deer, and they gave one bound to the roof and landed beside the big chimney.

"Good!" cried Claus, well pleased, and he slung the pack of toys over his shoulder and got into the chimney.

There was plenty of soot on the bricks, but he did not mind that, and by placing his hands and knees against the sides he crept downward until he had reached the fireplace. Leaping lightly over the smoldering coals he found himself in a large sitting-room, where a dim light was burning.

From this room two doorways led into smaller chambers. In one a woman lay asleep, with a baby beside her in a crib.

Claus laughed, but he did not laugh aloud for fear of waking the baby. Then he slipped a big doll from his pack and laid it in the crib. The little one smiled, as if it dreamed of the pretty plaything it was to find on the morrow, and Claus crept softly from the room and entered at the other doorway.

Here were two boys, fast asleep with their arms around each other's neck. Claus gazed at them lovingly a moment and then placed upon the bed a drum, two horns and a wooden elephant.

He did not linger, now that his work in this house was done, but climbed the chimney again and seated himself on his sledge.

"Can you find another chimney?" he asked the reindeer.

"Easily enough," replied Glossie and Flossie.

Down to the edge of the roof they raced, and then, without pausing, leaped through the air to the top of the next building, where a huge, old-fashioned chimney stood.

"Don't be so long, this time," called Flossie, "or we shall never get back to the Forest by daybreak."

Claus made a trip down this chimney also and found five children sleeping in the house, all of whom were quickly supplied with toys.

When he returned the deer sprang to the next roof, but on descending the chimney Claus found no children there at all. That was not often the case in this village, however, so he lost less time than you might suppose in visiting the dreary homes where there were no little ones.

When he had climbed down the chimneys of all the

houses in that village, and had left a toy for every sleeping child, Claus found that his great sack was not yet half emptied.

"Onward, friends!" he called to the deer; "we must seek another village."

So away they dashed, although it was long past midnight, and in a surprisingly short time they came to a large city, the largest Claus had ever visited since he began to make toys. But, nothing daunted by the throng of houses, he set to work at once and his beautiful steeds carried him rapidly from one roof to another, only the highest being beyond the leaps of the agile deer.

At last the supply of toys was exhausted and Claus seated himself in the sledge, with the empty sack at his feet, and turned the heads of Glossie and Flossie toward home.

Presently Flossie asked:

"What is that gray streak in the sky?"

"It is the coming dawn of day," answered Claus, surprised to find that it was so late.

"Good gracious!" exclaimed Glossie; "then we shall not be home by daybreak, and the Knooks will punish us and never let us come again."

"We must race for the Laughing Valley and make our best speed," returned Flossie; "so hold fast, friend Claus!"

Claus held fast and the next moment was flying so swiftly over the snow that he could not see the trees as they whirled past. Up hill and down dale, swift as an arrow shot from a bow they dashed, and Claus shut his eyes to keep the wind out of them and left the deer to find their own way.

It seemed to him they were plunging through space, but he was not at all afraid. The Knooks were severe masters, and must be obeyed at all hazards, and the gray streak in the sky was growing brighter every moment.

Finally the sledge came to a sudden stop and Claus, who

was taken unawares, tumbled from his seat into a snowdrift. As he picked himself up he heard the deer crying:

"Quick, friend, quick! Cut away our harness!"

He drew his knife and rapidly severed the cords, and then he wiped the moisture from his eyes and looked around him.

The sledge had come to a stop in the Laughing Valley, only a few feet, he found, from his own door. In the East the day was breaking, and turning to the edge of Burzee he saw Glossie and Flossie just disappearing in the Forest.

CHAPTER NINTH

"Santa Claus!"

CLAUS THOUGHT that none of the children would ever know where the toys came from which they found by their bedsides when they wakened the following morning. But kindly deeds are sure to bring fame, and fame has many wings to carry its tidings into far lands; so for miles and miles in every direction people were talking of Claus and his wonderful gifts to children. The sweet generousness of his work caused a few selfish folk to sneer, but even these were forced to admit their respect for a man so gentle-natured that he loved to devote his life to pleasing the helpless little ones of his race.

Therefore the inhabitants of every city and village had been eagerly watching the coming of Claus, and remarkable stories of his beautiful playthings were told the children to keep them patient and contented.

When, on the morning following the first trip of Claus with his deer, the little ones came running to their parents with the pretty toys they had found, and asked from whence they came, there was but one reply to the question.

"The good Claus must have been here, my darlings; for his are the only toys in all the world!"

"But how did he get in?" asked the children.

At this the fathers shook their heads, being themselves

unable to understand how Claus had gained admittance to their homes; but the mothers, watching the glad faces of their dear ones, whispered that the good Claus was no mortal man but assuredly a Saint, and they piously blessed his name for the happiness he had bestowed upon their children.

"A Saint," said one, with bowed head, "has no need to unlock doors if it pleases him to enter our homes."

And, afterward, when a child was naughty or disobedient, its mother would say:

"You must pray to the good Santa Claus for forgiveness. He does not like naughty children, and, unless you repent, he will bring you no more pretty toys."

But Santa Claus himself would not have approved this speech. He brought toys to the children because they were little and helpless, and because he loved them. He knew that the best of children were sometimes naughty, and that the naughty ones were often good. It is the way with children, the world over, and he would not have changed their natures had he possessed the power to do so.

And that is how our Claus became Santa Claus. It is possible for any man, by good deeds, to enshrine himself as a Saint in the hearts of the people.

CHAPTER TENTH

Christmas Eve

THE DAY that broke as Claus returned from his night ride with Glossie and Flossie brought to him a new trouble. Will Knook, the chief guardian of the deer, came to him, surly and ill-tempered, to complain that he had kept Glossie and Flossie beyond daybreak, in opposition to his orders.

"Yet it could not have been very long after daybreak," said Claus.

"It was one minute after," answered Will Knook, "and that is as bad as one hour. I shall set the stinging gnats on Glossie and Flossie, and they will thus suffer terribly for their disobedience."

"Don't do that!" begged Claus. "It was my fault."

But Will Knook would listen to no excuses, and went away grumbling and growling in his ill-natured way.

For this reason Claus entered the Forest to consult Necile about rescuing the good deer from punishment. To his delight he found his old friend, the Master Woodsman, seated in the circle of Nymphs.

Ak listened to the story of the night journey to the children and of the great assistance the deer had been to Claus by drawing his sledge over the frozen snow.

"I do not wish my friends to be punished if I can save

them," said the toy-maker, when he had finished the relation. "They were only one minute late, and they ran swifter than a bird flies to get home before daybreak."

Ak stroked his beard thoughtfully a moment, and then sent for the Prince of the Knooks, who rules all his people in Burzee, and also for the Queen of the Fairies and the Prince of the Ryls.

When all had assembled Claus told his story again, at Ak's command, and then the Master addressed the Prince of the Knooks, saying:

"The good work that Claus is doing among mankind deserves the support of every honest immortal. Already he is called a Saint in some of the towns, and before long the name of Santa Claus will be lovingly known in every home that is blessed with children. Moreover, he is a son of our Forest, so we owe him our encouragement. You, Ruler of the Knooks, have known him these many years; am I not right in saying he deserves our friendship?"

The Prince, crooked and sour of visage as all Knooks are, looked only upon the dead leaves at his feet and muttered: "You are the Master Woodsman of the World!"

Ak smiled, but continued, in soft tones: "It seems that the deer which are guarded by your people can be of great assistance to Claus, and as they seem willing to draw his sledge I beg that you will permit him to use their services whenever he pleases."

The Prince did not reply, but tapped the curled point of his sandal with the tip of his spear, as if in thought.

Then the Fairy Queen spoke to him in this way: "If you consent to Ak's request I will see that no harm comes to your deer while they are away from the Forest."

And the Prince of the Ryls added: "For my part I will allow to every deer that assists Claus the privilege of eating my casa plants, which give strength, and my grawle plants, which give fleetness of foot, and my marbon plants, which give long life."

And the Queen of the Nymphs said: "The deer which draw the sledge of Claus will be permitted to bathe in the Forest pool of Nares, which will give them sleek coats and wonderful beauty."

The Prince of the Knooks, hearing these promises, shifted uneasily on his seat, for in his heart he hated to refuse a request of his fellow immortals, although they were asking an unusual favor at his hands, and the Knooks are unaccustomed to granting favors of any kind. Finally he turned to his servants and said:

"Call Will Knook."

When surly Will came and heard the demands of the immortals he protested loudly against granting them.

"Deer are deer," said he, "and nothing but deer. Were they horses it would be right to harness them like horses. But no one harnesses deer because they are free, wild creatures, owing no service of any sort to mankind. It would degrade my deer to labor for Claus, who is only a man in spite of the friendship lavished on him by the immortals."

"You have heard," said the Prince to Ak. "There is truth in what Will says."

"Call Glossie and Flossie," returned the Master.

The deer were brought to the conference and Ak asked them if they objected to drawing the sledge for Claus.

"No, indeed!" replied Glossie; "we enjoyed the trip very much."

"And we tried to get home by daybreak," added Flossie, "but were unfortunately a minute too late."

"A minute lost at daybreak doesn't matter," said Ak. "You are forgiven for that delay."

"Provided it does not happen again," said the Prince of the Knooks, sternly.

"And will you permit them to make another journey with me?" asked Claus, eagerly.

The Prince reflected while he gazed at Will, who was scowling, and at the Master Woodsman, who was smiling.

Then he stood up and addressed the company as follows:

"Since you all urge me to grant the favor I will permit the deer to go with Claus once every year, on Christmas Eve, provided they always return to the Forest by daybreak. He may select any number he pleases, up to ten, to draw his sledge, and those shall be known among us as Reindeer, to distinguish them from the others. And they shall bathe in the Pool of Nares, and eat the casa and grawle and marbon plants and shall be under the especial protection of the Fairy Queen. And now cease scowling, Will Knook, for my words shall be obeyed!"

He

hobbled quickly away through the trees, to avoid the thanks of Claus and the approval of the other immortals, and Will, looking as cross as ever, followed him.

But Ak was satisfied, knowing that he could rely on the promise of the Prince, however grudgingly given; and Glossie and Flossie ran home, kicking up their heels delightedly at every step.

"When is Christmas Eve?" Claus asked the Master.

"In about ten days," he replied.

"Then I can not use the deer this year," said Claus, thoughtfully, "for I shall not have time enough to make my sackful of toys."

"The shrewd Prince foresaw that," responded Ak, "and therefore named Christmas Eve as the day you might use the deer, knowing it would cause you to lose an entire year."

"If I only had the toys the Awgwas stole from me," said Claus, sadly, "I could easily fill my sack for the children."

"Where are they?" asked the Master.

"I do not know," replied Claus, "but the wicked Awgwas probably hid them in the mountains."

Ak turned to the Fairy Queen.

"Can you find them?" he asked.

"I will try," she replied, brightly.

Then Claus went back to the Laughing Valley, to work as hard as he could, and a band of Fairies immediately flew to the mountain that had been haunted by the Awgwas and began a search for the stolen toys.

The Fairies, as we well know, possess wonderful powers; but the cunning Awgwas had hidden the toys in a deep cave and covered the opening with rocks, so no one could look in. Therefore all search for the missing playthings proved in vain for several days, and Claus, who sat at home waiting for news from the Fairies, almost despaired of getting the toys before Christmas Eve.

He worked hard every moment, but it took considerable time to carve out and to shape each toy and to paint it properly, so that on the morning before Christmas Eve only half of one small shelf above the window was filled with playthings ready for the children.

But on this morning the Fairies who were searching in the mountains had a new thought. They joined hands and moved in a straight line through the rocks that formed the mountain, beginning at the topmost peak and working downward, so that no spot could be missed by their bright eyes.

And at last they discovered the cave where the toys had been heaped up by the wicked Awgwas.

It did not take them long to burst open the mouth of the cave, and then each one seized as many toys as he could carry and they all flew to Claus and laid the treasure before him.

The good man was rejoiced to receive, just in the nick of time, such a store of playthings with which to load his sledge, and he sent word to Glossie and Flossie to be ready for the journey at nightfall.

With all his other labors he had managed to find time, since the last trip, to repair the harness and to strengthen his sledge, so that when the deer came to him at twilight he had no difficulty in harnessing them.

"We must go in another direction to-night," he told them, "where we shall find children I have never yet visited. And we must travel fast and work quickly, for my sack is full of toys and running over the brim!"

So, just as the moon arose, they dashed out of the Laughing Valley and across the plain and over the hills to the south. The air was sharp and frosty and the starlight touched the snowflakes and made them glitter like countless diamonds. The reindeer leaped onward with strong, steady bounds, and Claus' heart was so light and merry that he laughed and sang while the wind whistled past his ears:

> *"With a ho, ho, ho!*
> *And a ha, ha, ha!*
> *And a ho, ho! ha, ha, hee!*
> *Now away we go*
> *O'er the frozen snow,*
> *As merry as we can be!"*

Jack Frost heard him and came racing up with his nippers, but when he saw it was Claus he laughed and turned away again.

The mother owls heard him as he passed near a wood and stuck their heads out of the hollow places in the tree-trunks; but when they saw who it was they whispered to the owlets nestling near them that it was only Santa Claus carrying toys to the children. It is strange how much those mother owls know.

Claus stopped at some of the scattered farmhouses and climbed down the chimneys to leave presents for the babies. Soon after he reached a village and worked merrily for an hour distributing playthings among the sleeping little ones. Then away again he went, signing his joyous carol:

> *"Now away we go*
> *O'er the gleaming snow,*
> *While the deer run swift and free!*
> *For to girls and boys*
> *We carry the toys*
> *That will fill their hearts with glee!"*

The deer liked the sound of his deep bass voice and kept time to the song with their hoofbeats on the hard snow; but soon they stopped at another chimney and Santa Claus, with sparkling eyes and face brushed red by the wind, climbed down its smoky sides and left a present for every child the house contained.

It was a merry, happy night. Swiftly the deer ran, and busily their driver worked to scatter his gifts among the sleeping children.

But the sack was empty at last, and the sledge headed homeward; and now again the race with daybreak began. Glossie and Flossie had no mind to be rebuked a second time for tardiness, so they fled with a swiftness that enabled them to pass the gale on which the Frost King rode, and soon brought them to the Laughing Valley.

It is true when Claus released his steeds from their harness the eastern sky was streaked with gray, but Glossie and Flossie were deep in the Forest before day fairly broke.

Claus was so wearied with his night's work that he threw himself upon his bed and fell into a deep slumber, and while he slept the Christmas sun appeared in the sky and shone upon hundreds of happy homes where the sound of childish laughter proclaimed that Santa Claus had made them a visit.

God bless him! It was his first Christmas Eve, and for hundreds of years since then he has nobly fulfilled his mission to bring happiness to the hearts of little children.

CHAPTER ELEVENTH

How the First Stockings were Hung by the Chimney

WHEN YOU REMEMBER that no child, until Santa Claus began his travels, had ever known the pleasure of possessing a toy, you will understand how joy crept into the homes of those who had been favored with a visit from the good man, and how they talked of him day by day in loving tones and were honestly grateful for his kindly deeds. It is true that great warriors and mighty kings and clever scholars of that day were often spoken of by the people; but no one of them was so greatly beloved as Santa Claus, because none other was so unselfish as to devote himself to making others happy. For a generous deed lives longer than a great battle or a king's decree of a scholar's essay, because it spreads and leaves its mark on all nature and endures through many generations.

The bargain made with the Knook Prince changed the plans of Claus for all future time; for, being able to use the reindeer on but one night of each year, he decided to devote all the other days to the manufacture of playthings, and on Christmas Eve to carry them to the children of the world.

But a year's work would, he knew, result in a vast accumulation of toys, so he resolved to build a new sledge that would be larger and stronger and better-fitted for swift travel than the old and clumsy one.

His first act was to visit the Gnome King, with whom he made a bargain to exchange three drums, a trumpet and two dolls for a pair of fine steel runners, curled beautifully at the ends. For the Gnome King had children of his own, who, living in the hollows under the earth, in mines and caverns, needed something to amuse them.

In three days the steel runners were ready, and when Claus brought the playthings to the Gnome King, his Majesty was so greatly pleased with them that he presented Claus with a string of sweet-toned sleigh-bells, in addition to the runners.

"These will please Glossie and Flossie," said Claus, as he jingled the bells and listened to their merry sound. "But I should have two strings of bells, one for each deer."

"Bring me another trumpet and a toy cat," replied the King, "and you shall have a second string of bells like the first."

"It is a bargain!" cried Claus, and he went home again for the toys.

The new sledge was carefully built, the Knooks bringing plenty of strong but thin boards to use in its construction. Claus made a high, rounding dash-board to keep off the snow cast behind by the fleet hoofs of the deer; and he made high sides to the platform so that many toys could be carried, and finally he mounted the sledge upon the slender steel runners made by the Gnome King.

It was certainly a handsome sledge, and big and roomy. Claus painted it in bright colors, although no one was likely to see it during his midnight journeys, and when all was finished he sent for Glossie and Flossie to come and look at it.

The deer admired the sledge, but gravely declared it was too big and heavy for them to draw.

"We might pull it over the snow, to be sure," said Glossie; "but we would not pull it fast enough to enable us to visit the far-away cities and villages and return to the Forest by daybreak."

"Then I must add two more deer to my team," declared Claus, after a moment's thought.

"The Knook Prince allowed you as many as ten. Why not use them all?" asked Flossie. "Then we could speed like the lightning and leap to the highest roofs with ease."

"A team of ten reindeer!" cried Claus, delightedly. "That will be splendid. Please return to the Forest at once and select eight other deer as like yourselves as possible. And you must all eat of the casa plant, to become strong, and of the grawle plant, to become fleet of foot, and of the marbon plant, that you may live long to accompany me on my journeys. Likewise it will be well for you to bathe in the Pool of Nares, which the lovely Queen Zurline declares will render you rarely beautiful. Should you perform these duties faithfully there is no doubt that on next Christmas Eve my ten reindeer will be the most powerful and beautiful steeds the world has ever seen!"

So Glossie and Flossie went to the Forest to choose their mates, and Claus began to consider the question of a harness for them all.

In the end he called upon Peter Knook for assistance, for Peter's heart is as kind as his body is crooked, and he is remarkably shrewd, as well. And Peter agreed to furnish strips of tough leather for the harness.

This leather was cut from the skins of lions that had reached such an advanced age that they died naturally, and on one side was tawny hair while the other side was cured to the softness of velvet by the deft Knooks. When Claus received these strips of leather he sewed them neatly into a harness for the ten reindeer, and it proved strong and serviceable and lasted him for many years.

The harness and sledge were prepared at odd times, for Claus devoted most of his days to the making of toys. These were now much better than the first ones had been, for the immortals often came to his house to watch him work and to offer suggestions. It was Necile's idea to make some of the dolls say "papa" and "mama." It was a thought of the Knooks to put a squeak inside the lambs, so that when a child squeezed them they would say "baa-a-a-a!" And the Fairy Queen advised Claus to put whistles in the birds, so they could be made to sing, and wheels on the horses, so children could draw them around. Many animals perished in the Forest, from one cause or another, and their fur was brought to Claus that he might cover with it the small images of beasts he made for playthings. A merry Ryl suggested that Claus make a donkey with a nodding head, which he did, and afterward found that it amused the little ones immensely. And so the toys grew in beauty and attractiveness every day, until they were the wonder of even the immortals.

When another Christmas Eve drew near there was a monster load of beautiful gifts for the children ready to be loaded upon the big sledge. Claus filled three sacks to the brim, and tucked every corner of the sledge-box full of toys besides.

Then, at twilight, the ten reindeer appeared and Flossie introduced them all to Claus. They were Racer and Pacer, Reckless and Speckless, Fearless and Peerless, and Ready and Steady, who, with Glossie and Flossie, made up the ten who have traversed the world these hundreds of years with their generous master. They were all exceedingly beautiful, with slender limbs, spreading antlers, velvety dark eyes and smooth coats of fawn color spotted with white.

Claus loved them at once, and has loved them ever since, for they are loyal friends and have rendered him priceless service.

The new harness fitted them nicely and soon they were all fastened to the sledge by twos, with Glossie and Flossie in the lead. These wore the strings of sleigh-bells, and were so delighted with the music they made that they kept prancing up and down to make the bells ring.

Claus now seated himself in the sledge, drew a warm robe over his knees and his fur cap over his ears, and cracked his long whip as a signal to start.

Instantly the ten leaped forward and were away like the wind, while jolly Claus laughed gleefully to see them run and shouted a song in his big, hearty voice:

"With a ho, ho, ho!
And a ha, ha, ha!
And a ho, ho, ha, ha, hee!
Now away we go

O'er the frozen snow,
As merry as we can be!
There are many joys
In our load of toys,

As many a child will know;
We'll scatter them wide
On our wild night ride
O'er the crisp and sparkling snow!"

Now it was on this same Christmas Eve that little Margot and her brother Dick and her cousins Ned and Sara, who were visiting at Margot's house, came in from making a snow man, with their clothes damp, their mittens dripping and their shoes and stockings wet through and through. They were not scolded, for Margot's mother knew the snow was melting, but they were sent early to bed that their clothes might be hung over chairs to dry. The shoes were placed on the red tiles of the hearth, where the heat from the hot embers would strike them, and the stockings were carefully hung in a row by the chimney, directly over the fireplace. That was the reason Santa Claus noticed them when he came down the chimney that night and all the household were fast asleep. He was in a tremendous hurry and seeing the stockings all belonged to children he quickly stuffed his toys into them and dashed up the chimney again, appearing on the roof so suddenly that the reindeer were astonished at his agility.

"I wish they would all hang up their stockings," he thought, as he drove to the next chimney. "It would save me a lot of time and I could then visit more children before daybreak."

When Margot and Dick and Ned and Sara jumped out of bed next morning and ran downstairs to get their stockings from the fireplace they were filled with delight to find the toys from Santa Claus inside them. In fact, I think they found more presents in their stockings than any other children of that city had received, for Santa Claus was in a hurry and did not stop to count the toys.

Of course they told all their little friends about it, and of course every one of them decided to hang his own stockings by the fireplace the next Christmas Eve. Even Bessie Blithesome, who made a visit to that city with her father, the great Lord of Lerd, heard the story from the children and hung her own pretty stockings by the chimney when she returned home at Christmas time.

On his next trip Santa Claus found so many stockings hung up in anticipation of his visit that he could fill them in a jiffy and be away again in half the time required to hunt the children up and place the toys by their bedsides.

The custom grew year after year, and has always been a great help to Santa Claus. And, with so many children to visit, he surely needs all the help we are able to give him.

CHAPTER TWELFTH

The First Christmas Tree

CLAUS HAS ALWAYS KEPT his promise to the Knooks by returning to the Laughing Valley by daybreak, but only the swiftness of his reindeer has enabled him to do this, for he travels over all the world.

He loved his work and he loved the brisk night ride on his sledge and the gay tinkle of the sleigh-bells. On that first trip with the ten reindeer only Glossie and Flossie wore bells; but each year thereafter for eight years Claus carried presents to the children of the Gnome King, and that good-natured monarch gave him in return a string of bells at each visit, so that finally every one of the ten deer was supplied, and you may imagine what a merry tune the bells played as the sledge sped over the snow.

The children's stockings were so long that it required a great many toys to fill them, and soon Claus found there were other things besides toys that children love. So he sent some of the Fairies, who were always his good friends, into the Tropics, from whence they returned with great bags full of oranges and bananas which they had plucked from the trees. And other Fairies flew to the wonderful Valley of Phunnyland, where delicious candies and bonbons grow thickly on the bushes, and returned laden with many boxes of sweetmeats for the little ones. These things Santa Claus, on each Christmas Eve, placed in the long stockings, together with his toys, and the children were glad to get them, you may be sure.

There are also warm countries where there is no snow in winter, but Claus and his reindeer visited them as well as the colder climes, for there were little wheels inside the runners of his sledge which permitted it to run as smoothly over bare ground as on the snow. And the children who lived in the warm countries learned to know the name of Santa Claus as well as those who lived nearer to the Laughing Valley.

Once, just as the reindeer were ready to start on their yearly trip, a Fairy came to Claus and told him of three little children who lived beneath a rude tent of skins on a broad plain where there were no trees whatever. These poor babies were miserable and unhappy, for their parents were ignorant people who neglected them sadly. Claus resolved to visit these children before he returned home, and during his ride he picked up the bushy top of a pine tree which the wind had broken off and placed it in his sledge.

It was nearly morning when the deer stopped before the lonely tent of skins where the poor children lay asleep. Claus at once planted the bit of pine tree in the sand and stuck many candles on the branches. Then he hung some of his prettiest toys on the tree, as well as several bags of candies. It did not take long to do all this, for Santa Claus works quickly, and when all was ready he lighted the candles and, thrusting his head in at the opening of the tent, he shouted:

"Merry Christmas, little ones!"

With that he leaped into his sledge and was out of sight before the children, rubbing the sleep from their eyes, could come out to see who had called them.

You can imagine the wonder and joy of those little ones, who had never in their lives known a real pleasure before, when they saw the tree, sparkling with lights that shone brilliant in the gray dawn and hung with toys enough to make them happy for years to come! They joined hands and danced around the tree, shouting and laughing, until they were obliged to pause for breath. And their parents, also, came out to look and wonder, and thereafter had more respect and consideration for their children, since Santa Claus had honored them with such beautiful gifts.

The idea of the Christmas tree pleased Claus, and so the following year he carried many of them in his sledge and set them up in the homes of poor people who seldom saw trees, and placed candles and toys on the branches. Of course he could not carry enough trees in one load of all who wanted them, but in some homes the fathers were able to get trees and have them all ready for Santa Claus when he arrived; and these the good Claus always decorated as prettily as possible and hung with toys enough for all the children who came to see the tree lighted.

These novel ideas and the generous manner in which they were carried out made the children long for that one night in the year when their friend Santa Claus should visit them, and as such anticipation is very pleasant and comforting, the little ones gleaned much happiness by wondering what would happen when Santa Claus next arrived.

Perhaps you remember that stern Baron Braun who once drove Claus from his castle and forbade him to visit his children? Well, many years afterward, when the old Baron was dead and his son ruled in his place, the new Baron Braun came to the house of Claus with his train of knights and pages and henchmen and, dismounting from his charger, bared his head humbly before the friend of children.

"My father did not know your goodness and worth," he said, "and therefore threatened to hang you from the castle walls. But I have children of my own who long for a visit from Santa Claus, and I have come to beg that you will favor them hereafter as you do other children."

Claus was pleased with this speech, for Castle Braun was the only place he had never visited, and he gladly promised to bring presents to the Baron's children the next Christmas Eve.

The Baron went away contented, and Claus kept his promise faithfully.

Thus did this man, through very goodness, conquer the hearts of all; and it is no wonder he was ever merry and gay, for there was no home in the wide world where he was not welcomed more royally than any king.

CHAPTER FIRST

The Mantle of Immortality

AND NOW WE come to a turning-point in the career of Santa Claus, and it is my duty to relate the most remarkable that has happened since the world began or mankind was created.

We have followed the life of Claus from the time he was found a helpless infant by the Wood-Nymph Necile and reared to manhood in the great Forest of Burzee. And we know how he began to make toys for children and how, with the assistance and good-will of the immortals, he was able to distribute them to the little ones throughout the world.

For many years he carried on this noble work; for the simple, hard-working life he led gave him perfect health and strength. And doubtless a man can live longer in the beautiful Laughing Valley, where there are no cares and everything is peaceful and merry, than in any other part of the world.

But when many years had rolled away Santa Claus grew old. The long beard of golden brown that once covered his cheeks and chin gradually became gray, and finally turned to pure white. His hair was white, too, and there were wrinkles at the corners of his eyes, which showed plainly when he laughed. He had never been a very tall man, and now he became fat, and waddled very much like a duck when he walked. But in spite of these things he remained as lively as ever, and was just as jolly and gay, and his kind eyes sparkled as brightly as they did that first day when he came to the Laughing Valley.

Yet a time is sure to come when every mortal who has grown old and lived his life is required to leave this world for another; so it is no wonder that, after Santa Claus had driven his reindeer on many and many a Christmas Eve, those stanch friends finally whispered among themselves that they had probably drawn his sledge for the last time.

Then all the Forest of Burzee became sad and all the Laughing Valley was hushed; for every living thing that had known Claus had used to love him and to brighten at the sound of his footsteps or the notes of his merry whistle.

No doubt the old man's strength was at last exhausted, for he made no more toys, but lay on his bed as in a dream.

The Nymph Necile, she who had reared him and been his foster-mother, was still youthful and strong and beautiful, and it seemed to her but a short time since this aged, gray-bearded man had lain in her arms and smiled on her with his innocent, baby lips.

In this is shown the difference between mortals and immortals.

It was fortunate that the great Ak came to the Forest at this time. Necile sought him with troubled eyes and told him of the fate that threatened their friend Claus.

At once the Master became grave, and he leaned upon his ax and stroked his grizzled beard thoughtfully for many minutes. Then suddenly he stood up straight, and poised his powerful head with firm resolve, and stretched out his great right arm as if determined on doing some mighty deed. For a thought had come to him so grand in its conception that all the world might well bow before the Master Woodsman and honor his name forever!

It is well known that when the great Ak once undertakes to do a thing he never hesitates an instant. Now he summoned his fleetest messengers, and sent them in a flash to many parts of the earth. And when they were gone he turned to the anxious Necile and comforted her, saying:

"Be of good heart, my child; our friend still lives. And now run to your Queen and tell her that I have summoned a council of all the immortals of the world to meet with me here in Burzee this night. If they obey, and harken unto my words, Claus will drive his reindeer for countless ages yet to come."

At midnight there was a wondrous scene in the ancient Forest of Burzee, where for the first time in many centuries the rulers of the immortals who inhabit the earth were gathered together.

There was the Queen of the Water Sprites, whose beautiful form was as clear as crystal but continually dripped water on the bank of moss where she sat. And beside her was the King of the Sleep Fays, who carried a wand from the end of which a fine dust fell all around, so that no mortal could keep awake long enough to see him, as mortal eyes were sure to close in sleep as soon as the dust filled them. And next to him sat the Gnome King, whose people inhabit all that region under the earth's surface, where they guard the precious metals and the jewel stones that lie buried in rock and ore. At his right hand stood the King of the Sound Imps, who had wings on his feet, for his people are swift to carry all sounds that are made. When they are busy they carry the sounds but short distances, for there are many of them; but sometimes they speed with the sounds to places miles and miles away from where they are made. The King of the Sound Imps had an anxious and care-worn face, for most people have no consideration for his Imps and, especially the boys and girls, make a great many unnecessary sounds which the Imps are obliged to carry when they might be better employed.

The next in the circle of immortals was the King of the Wind Demons, slender of frame, restless and uneasy at being confined to one place for even an hour. Once in a while he would leave his place and circle around the glade, and each time he did this the Fairy Queen was obliged to untangle the flowing locks of her golden hair and tuck them back of her pink ears. But she did not complain, for it was not often that the King of the Wind Demons came into the heart of the Forest. After the Fairy Queen, whose home you know was in old Burzee, came the King of the Light Elves, with his two Princes, Flash and Twilight, at his back. He never went anywhere without his Princes, for they were so mischievous that he dared not let them wander alone.

Prince Flash bore a lightning-bolt in his right hand and a horn of gunpowder in his left, and his bright eyes roved constantly around, as if he longed to use his blinding flashes. Prince Twilight held a great snuffer in one hand and a big black cloak in the other, and it is well known that unless Twilight is carefully watched the snuffers or the cloak will throw everything into darkness, and Darkness is the greatest enemy the King of the Light Elves has.

In addition to the immortals I have named were the King of the Knooks, who had come from his home in the jungles of India; and the King of the Ryls, who lived among the gay flowers and luscious fruits of Valencia. Sweet Queen Zurline of the Wood-Nymphs completed the circle of immortals.

But in the center of the circle sat three others who possessed powers so great that all the Kings and Queens showed them reverence.

These were Ak, the Master Woodsman of the World, who rules the forests and the orchards and the groves; and Kern, the Master Husbandman of the World, who rules the grain fields and the meadows and the gardens; and Bo, the Master Mariner of the World, who rules the seas and all the craft that float thereon. And all other immortals are more or less subject to these three.

When all had assembled, the Master Woodsman of the World stood up to address them, since he himself had summoned them to the council.

Very clearly he told them the story of Claus, beginning at the time when as a babe he had been adopted a child of the Forest, and telling of his noble and generous nature and his life-long labors to make children happy.

"And now," said Ak, "when he has won the love of all the world, the Spirit of Death is hovering over him. Of all men who have inhabited the earth none other so well deserves immortality, for such a life can not be spared so long as there are children of mankind to miss him and to grieve over his loss. We immortals are the servants of the world, and to serve the world we were permitted in the Beginning to exist. But what one of us is more worthy of immortality than this man Claus, who so sweetly ministers to the little children?"

He paused and glanced around the circle, to find every immortal listening to him eagerly and nodding approval. Finally the King of the Wind Demons, who had been whistling softly to himself, cried out:

"What is your desire, O Ak?"

"To bestow upon Claus the Mantle of Immortality!" said Ak, boldly.

That this demand was wholly unexpected was proved by

the immortals springing to their feet and looking into each other's face with dismay and then upon Ak with wonder. For it was a grave matter, this parting with the Mantle of Immortality.

The Queen of the Water Sprites spoke in her low, clear voice, and the words sounded like raindrops splashing upon a window-pane.

"In all the world there is but one Mantle of Immortality," she said.

The King of the Sound Fays added:

"It has existed since the Beginning, and no mortal has ever dared to claim it."

And the Master Mariner of the World arose and stretched his limbs, saying:

"Only by the vote of every immortal can it be bestowed upon a mortal."

"I know all this," answered Ak, quietly. "But the Mantle exists, and if it was created, as you say, in the Beginning, it was because the Supreme Master knew that some day it would be required. Until now no mortal has deserved it, but who among you dares deny that the good Claus deserves it? Will you not all vote to bestow it upon him?"

They were silent, still looking upon one another questioningly.

"Of what use is the Mantle of Immortality unless it is worn?" demanded Ak. "What will it profit any one of us to allow it to remain in its lonely shrine for all time to come?"

"Enough!" cried the Gnome King, abruptly. "We will vote on the matter, yes or no. For my part, I say yes!"

"And I!" said the Fairy Queen, promptly, and Ak rewarded her with a smile.

"My people in Burzee tell me they have learned to love him; therefore I vote to give Claus the Mantle," said the King of the Ryls.

"He is already a comrade of the Knooks," announced the ancient King of that band. "Let him have immortality!"

"Let him have it—let him have it!" sighed the King of the Wind Demons.

"Why not?" asked the King of the Sleep Fays. "He never disturbs the slumbers my people allow humanity. Let the good Claus be immortal!"

"I do not object," said the King of the Sound Imps.

"Nor I," murmured the Queen of the Water Sprites.

"If Claus does not receive the Mantle it is clear none other can ever claim it," remarked the King of the Light Elves, "so let us have done with the thing for all time."

"The Wood-Nymphs were first to adopt him," said Queen Zurline. "Of course I shall vote to make him immortal."

Ak now turned to the Master Husbandman of the World, who held up his right arm and said "Yes!"

And the Master Mariner of the World did likewise, after which Ak, with sparkling eyes and smiling face, cried out:

"I thank you, fellow immortals! For all have voted 'yes,' and so to our dear Claus shall fall the one Mantle of Immortality that it is in our power to bestow!"

"Let us fetch it at once," said the Fay King; "I'm in a hurry."

They bowed assent, and instantly the Forest glade was deserted. But in a place midway between the earth and the sky was suspended a gleaming crypt of gold and platinum, aglow with soft lights shed from the facets of countless gems. Within a high dome hung the precious Mantle of Immortality, and each immortal placed a hand on the hem of the splendid Robe and said, as with one voice:

"We bestow this Mantle upon Claus, who is called the Patron Saint of Children!"

At this the Mantle came away from its lofty crypt, and they carried it to the house in the Laughing Valley.

The Spirit of Death was crouching very near to the bedside

of Claus, and as the immortals approached she sprang up and motioned them back with an angry gesture. But when her eyes fell upon the Mantle they bore, she shrank away with a low moan of disappointment and quitted that house forever.

Softly and silently the immortal Band dropped upon Claus the precious Mantle, and it closed about him and sank into the outlines of his body and disappeared from view. It became a part of his being, and neither mortal nor immortal might ever take it from him.

Then the Kings and Queens who had wrought this great deed dispersed to their various homes, and all were well contented that they had added another immortal to their Band.

And Claus slept on, the red blood of everlasting life coursing swiftly through his veins; and on his brow was a tiny drop of water that had fallen from the ever-melting gown of the Queen of the Water Sprites, and over his lips hovered a tender kiss that had been left by the sweet Nymph Necile. For she had stolen in when the others were gone to gaze with rapture upon the immortal form of her foster son.

CHAPTER SECOND

When the World Grew Old

THE NEXT MORNING, when Santa Claus opened his eyes and gazed around the familiar room, which he had feared he might never see again, he was astonished to find his old strength renewed and to feel the red blood of perfect health coursing through his veins. He sprang from his bed and stood where the bright sunshine came in through his window and flooded him with its merry, dancing rays. He did not then understand what had happened to restore to him the vigor of youth, but in spite of the fact that his beard remained the color of snow and that wrinkles still lingered in the corners of his bright eyes, old Santa Claus felt as brisk and merry as a boy of sixteen, and was soon whistling contentedly as he busied himself fashioning new toys.

Then Ak came to him and told of the Mantle of Immortality and how Claus had won it through his love for little children.

It made old Santa look grave for a moment to think he had been so favored; but it also made him glad to realize that now he need never fear being parted from his dear ones. At once he began preparations for making a remarkable assortment of pretty and amusing playthings, and in larger quantities than ever before; for now that he might always devote himself to this work he decided that no child in the world, poor or rich, should hereafter go without a Christmas gift if he could manage to supply it.

The world was new in the days when dear old Santa Claus first began toy-making and won, by his loving deeds, the Mantle of Immortality. And the task of supplying cheering words, sympathy and pretty playthings to all the young of his race did not seem a difficult undertaking at all. But every year more and more children were born into the world, and these, when they grew up, began spreading slowly over all the face of the earth, seeking new homes; so that Santa Claus found each year that his journeys must extend farther and farther from the Laughing Valley, and that the packs of toys must be made larger and ever larger.

 So at length he took counsel with his fellow immortals how his work might keep pace with the increasing number of children that none might be neglected. And the immortals were so greatly interested in his labors that they gladly rendered him their assistance. Ak gave him his man Kilter, "the silent and swift." And the Knook Prince gave him Peter, who was more crooked and less surly than any of his brothers. And the Ryl Prince gave him Nuter, the sweetest tempered Ryl ever known. And the Fairy Queen gave him Wisk, that tiny, mischievous but lovable Fairy who knows today almost as many children as does Santa Claus himself.

With these people to help make the toys and to keep his house in order and to look after the sledge and the harness,

Santa Claus found it much easier to prepare his yearly load of gifts, and his days began to follow one another smoothly and pleasantly.

Yet after a few generations his worries were renewed, for it was remarkable how the number of people continued to grow, and how many more children there were every year to be served. When the people filled all the cities and lands of one country they wandered into another part of the world; and the men cut down the trees in many of the great forests that had been ruled by Ak, and with the wood they built new cities, and where the forests had been were fields of grain and herds of browsing cattle.

You might think the Master Woodsman would rebel at the loss of his forests; but not so. The wisdom of Ak was mighty and farseeing.

"The world was made for men," said he to Santa Claus, "and I have but guarded the forests until men needed them for their use. I am glad my strong trees can furnish shelter for men's weak bodies, and warm them through the cold winters. But I hope they will not cut down all the trees, for mankind needs the shelter of the woods in summer as much as the warmth of blazing logs in winter. And, however crowded the world may grow, I do not think men will ever come to Burzee, nor to the Great Black Forest, nor to the wooded wilderness of Braz; unless they seek their shades for pleasure and not to destroy their giant trees."

By and by people made ships from the tree-trunks and

crossed over oceans and built cities in far lands; but the oceans made little difference to the journeys of Santa Claus. His reindeer sped over the waters as swiftly as over land, and his sledge headed from east to west and followed in the wake of the sun. So that as the earth rolled slowly over Santa Claus had all of twenty-four hours to encircle it each Christmas Eve, and the speedy reindeer enjoyed these wonderful journeys more and more.

So year after year, and generation after generation, and century after century, the world grew older and the people became more numerous and the labors of Santa Claus steadily increased. The fame of his good deeds spread to every household where children dwelt. And all the little ones loved him dearly; and the fathers and mothers honored him for the happiness he had given them when they too were young; and the aged grandsires and granddames remembered him with tender gratitude and blessed his name.

CHAPTER THIRD

The Deputies of Santa Claus

HOWEVER, there was one evil following in the path of civilization that caused Santa Claus a vast amount of trouble before he discovered a way to overcome it. But, fortunately, it was the last trial he was forced to undergo.

One Christmas Eve, when his reindeer had leaped to the top of a new building, Santa Claus was surprised to find that the chimney had been built much smaller than usual. But he had no time to think about it just then, so he drew in his breath and made himself as small as possible and slid down the chimney.

"I ought to be at the bottom by this time," he thought, as he continued to slip downward; but no fireplace of any sort met his view, and by and by he reached the very end of the chimney, which was in the cellar.

"This is odd!" he reflected, much puzzled by this experience. "If there is no fireplace, what on earth is the chimney good for?"

Then he began to climb out again, and found it hard work —the space being so small. And on his way up he noticed a thin, round pipe sticking through the side of the chimney, but could not guess what it was for.

Finally he reached the roof and said to the reindeer:

"There was no need of my going down that chimney, for I could find no fireplace through which to enter the house. I fear the children who live there must go without playthings this Christmas."

Then he drove on, but soon came to another new house with a small chimney. This caused Santa Claus to shake his head doubtfully, but he tried the chimney, nevertheless, and found it exactly like the other. Moreover, he nearly stuck fast in the narrow flue and tore his jacket trying to get out again; so, although he came to several such chimneys that night, he did not venture to descend any more of them.

"What in the world are people thinking of, to build such useless chimneys?" he exclaimed. "In all the years I have traveled with my reindeer I have never seen the like before."

True enough; but Santa Claus had not then discovered that stoves had been invented and were fast coming into use. When he did find it out he wondered how the builders of those houses could have so little consideration for him, when they knew very well it was his custom to climb down chimneys and enter houses by way of the fireplaces. Perhaps the men who built those houses had outgrown their own love for toys, and were indifferent whether Santa Claus called on their children or not. Whatever the explanation might be, the poor children were forced to bear the burden of grief and disappointment.

The following year Santa Claus found more and more of the new-fashioned chimneys that had no fireplaces, and the next year still more. The third year, so numerous had the narrow chimneys become, he even had a few toys left in his sledge that he was unable to give away, because he could not get to the children.

The matter had now become so serious that it worried the good man greatly, and he decided to talk it over with Kilter and Peter and Nuter and Wisk.

Kilter already knew something about it, for it had been his duty to run around to all the houses, just before Christmas, and gather up the notes and letters to Santa Claus that the children had written, telling what they wished put in their stockings or hung on their Christmas trees. But Kilter was a silent fellow, and seldom spoke of what he saw in the cities and villages. The others were very indignant.

"Those people act as if they do not wish their children to be made happy!" said sensible Peter, in a vexed tone. "The idea of shutting out such a generous friend to their little ones!"

"But it is my intention to make children happy whether their parents wish it or not," returned Santa Claus. "Years ago, when I first began making toys, children were even more neglected by their parents than they are now; so I have learned to pay no attention to thoughtless or selfish parents, but to consider only the longings of childhood."

"You are right, my master," said Nuter, the Ryl; "many children would lack a friend if you did not consider them, and try to make them happy."

"Then," declared the laughing Wisk, "we must abandon any thought of using these new-fashioned chimneys, but become burglars, and break into the houses some other way."

"What way?" asked Santa Claus.

"Why, walls of brick and wood and plaster are nothing to

Fairies. I can easily pass through them whenever I wish, and so can Peter and Nuter and Kilter. Is it not so, comrades?"

"I often pass through the walls when I gather up the letters," said Kilter, and that was a long speech for him, and so surprised Peter and Nuter that their big round eyes nearly popped out of their heads.

"Therefore," continued the Fairy, "you may as well take us with you on your next journey, and when we come to one of those houses with stoves instead of fireplaces we will distribute the toys to the children without the need of using a chimney."

"That seems to me a good plan," replied Santa Claus, well pleased at having solved the problem. "We will try it next year."

That was how the Fairy, the Pixie, the Knook and the Ryl all rode in the sledge with their master the following Christmas Eve; and they had no trouble at all in entering the new-fashioned houses and leaving toys for the children that lived in them.

And their deft services not only relieved Santa Claus of much labor, but enabled him to complete his own work more quickly than usual, so that the merry party found themselves at home with an empty sledge a full hour before daybreak.

The only drawback to the journey was that the mischievous

Wisk persisted in tickling the reindeer with a long feather, to see them jump; and Santa Claus found it necessary to watch him every minute and to tweak his long ears once or twice to make him behave himself.

But, taken all together, the trip was a great success, and to this day the four little folk always accompany Santa Claus on his yearly ride and help him in the distribution of his gifts.

But the indifference of parents, which had so annoyed the good Saint, did not continue very long, and Santa Claus soon found they were really anxious he should visit their homes on Christmas Eve and leave presents for their children.

So, to lighten his task, which was fast becoming very difficult indeed, old Santa decided to ask the parents to assist him.

"Get your Christmas trees all ready for my coming," he said to them; "and then I shall be able to leave the presents without loss of time, and you can put them on the trees when I am gone."

And to others he said: "See that the children's stockings are hung up in readiness for my coming, and then I can fill them as quick as a wink."

And often, when parents were kind and good-natured, Santa Claus would simply fling down his package of gifts and leave the fathers and mothers to fill the stockings after he had darted away in his sledge.

"I will make all loving parents my deputies!" cried the jolly old fellow, "and they shall help me do my work. For in this way I shall save many precious minutes and few children need be neglected for lack of time to visit them."

Besides carrying around the big packs in his swift-flying sledge old Santa began to send great heaps of toys to the toy-shops, so that if parents wanted larger supplies for their children they could easily get them; and if any children were, by chance, missed by Santa Claus on his yearly rounds, they could go to the toy-shops and get enough to make them happy and contented. For the loving friend of the little ones decided that no child, if he could help it, should long for toys in vain. And the toy-shops also proved convenient whenever a child fell ill, and needed a new toy to amuse it; and sometimes, on birthdays, the fathers and mothers go to the toy-shops and get pretty gifts for their children in honor of the happy event.

Perhaps you will now understand how, in spite of the bigness of the world, Santa Claus is able to supply all the children with beautiful gifts. To be sure, the old gentleman is rarely seen in these days; but it is not because he tries to keep out of sight, I assure you. Santa Claus is the same loving friend of children that in the old days used to play and romp with them by the hour; and I know he would love to do the same now, if he had the time. But, you see, he is so busy all the year making toys, and so hurried on that one night when he visits our homes with his packs, that he comes and goes among us like a flash; and it is almost impossible to catch a glimpse of him.

And, although there are millions and millions more children in the world than there used to be, Santa Claus has never been known to complain of their increasing numbers.

"The more the merrier!" he cries, with his jolly laugh; and the only difference to him is the fact that his little workmen have to make their busy fingers fly faster every year to satisfy the demands of so many little ones.

"In all this world there is nothing so beautiful as a happy child," says good old Santa Claus; and if he had his way the children would all be beautiful, for all would be happy.

A KIDNAPPED SANTA CLAUS

ILLUSTRATED BY FREDERICK
RICHARDSON

THE DELINEATOR

FOR DECEMBER 1904

CONDUCTED BY CHARLES DWYER

CONTENTS

PUBLISHED BY THE BUTTERICK PUBLISHING CO., LIMITED

Table of Contents from The Delineator, *December 1904. "A Kidnapped Santa Claus" is listed in the right column toward the top.*

EDITOR'S NOTE: "A Kidnapped Santa Claus" was written two years after The Life and Adventures of Santa Claus. *It initially appeared in the December 1904 edition of* The Delineator Magazine, *under the "Stories and Pastimes for Children" section. The magazine, which ran from the 1870s through the late 1930s and variously called itself "A Journal of Fashion, Culture and Fine Arts," and "An Illustrated Magazine of Literature and Fashion," featured several more of Baum's children's stories the following year as part of his "Animal Fairy Tales."*

A KIDNAPPED SANTA CLAUS

BY L. FRANK BAUM, Author of "The Wizard of Oz"

WITH DRAWINGS BY FRED RICHARDSON

SANTA CLAUS LIVES in the Laughing Valley, where stands the big, rambling castle in which his toys are manufactured. His workmen, selected from the Ryls, Knooks, Pixies and Fairies, live with him, and every one is as busy as can be from one year's end to another.

It is called the Laughing Valley because everything there is happy and gay. The brook chuckles to itself as it leaps rollicking between its green banks; the wind whistles merrily in the trees; the sunbeams dance lightly over the soft grass, and the violets and wild-flowers look smilingly up from their green nests. To laugh one needs to be happy; to be happy one needs to be content. And throughout the Laughing Valley of Santa Claus contentment reigns supreme.

On one side is the mighty Forest of Burzee. At the other side stands the huge mountain that contains the Caves of the Daemons. And between them the Valley lies smiling and peaceful.

One would think that our good old Santa Claus, who devotes his days to making children happy, would have no enemies on all the earth; and, as a matter of fact, for a long period of time he encountered nothing but love wherever he might go.

But the Daemons who live in the mountain caves grew to hate Santa Claus very much, and all for the simple reason that he made children happy.

The Caves of the Daemons are five in number. A broad pathway leads up to the first cave, which is a finely arched cavern at the foot of the mountain, the entrance being beautifully carved and decorated. In it resides the Daemon of Selfishness. Back of this is another cavern inhabited by the Daemon of Envy. The cave of the Daemon of Hatred is next in order, and through this one passes to the home of the Daemon of Malice—situated in a dark and fearful cave in the very heart of the mountain. I do not know what lies beyond this. Some say there are terrible pitfalls leading to death and destruction, and this may very well be true. However, from each one of the four caves mentioned there is a small, narrow tunnel leading to the fifth cave—a cozy little room occupied by the Daemon of Repentance. And as the rocky floors of these passages are well worn by the track of passing feet, I judge that many wanderers in the Caves of the Daemons have escaped through the tunnels to the abode of the Daemon of Repentance, who is said to be a pleasant sort of fellow who gladly opens for one a little door admitting you into fresh air and sunshine again.

Well, these Daemons of the Caves, thinking they had great cause to dislike old Santa Claus, held a meeting one day to discuss the matter.

"I'm really getting lonesome," said the Daemon of Selfishness. "For Santa Claus distributes so many pretty Christmas gifts to all the children that they become happy and generous, through his example, and keep away from my cave."

"I'm having the same trouble," rejoined the Daemon of Envy. "The little ones seem quite content with Santa Claus, and there are few, indeed, that I can coax to become envious."

"And that makes it bad for me!" declared the Daemon of

Hatred. "For if no children pass through the Caves of Selfishness and Envy, none can get to *my* cavern."

"Or to mine," added the Daemon of Malice.

"For my part," said the Daemon of Repentance, "it is easily seen that if children do not visit your caves they have no need to visit mine; so I am quite as neglected as you are."

"And all because of this person they call Santa Claus!" exclaimed the Daemon of Envy. "He is simply ruining our business, and something must be done at once."

To this they readily agreed; but what to do was another and more difficult matter to settle. They knew that Santa Claus worked all through the year at his castle in the Laughing Valley, preparing the gifts he was to distribute on Christmas Eve; and at first they resolved to try to tempt him into their caves, that they might lead him on to the terrible pitfalls that ended in destruction.

So the very next day, while Santa Claus was busily at work, surrounded by his little band of assistants, the Daemon of Selfishness came to him and said:

"These toys are wonderfully bright and pretty. Why do you not keep them for yourself? It's a pity to give them to those noisy boys and fretful girls, who break and destroy them so quickly."

"Nonsense!" cried the old graybeard, his bright eyes twinkling merrily as he turned toward the tempting Daemon; "the boys and girls are never so noisy and fretful after receiving my presents, and if I can make them happy for one day in the year I am quite content."

So the Daemon went back to the others, who awaited him in their caves, and said:

"I have failed, for Santa Claus is not at all selfish."

The following day the Daemon of Envy visited Santa Claus. Said he: "The toy-shops are full of playthings quite as pretty as those you are making. What a shame it is that they should interfere with your business! They make toys by machinery much quicker than you can make them by hand; and they sell them for money, while you get nothing at all for your work."

But Santa Claus refused to be envious of the toy-shops.

"I HAVE BAD NEWS FOR YOU," SAID THE DAEMON. "THEN RUN AWAY LIKE A GOOD FELLOW," ANSWERED SANTA.

"I can supply the little ones but once a year—on Christmas Eve," he answered; "for the children are many, and I am but one. And as my work is one of love and kindness I would be ashamed to receive money for my little gifts. But throughout all the year the children must be amused in some way, and so the toy-shops are able to bring much happiness to my little friends. I like the toy-shops, and am glad to see them prosper."

In spite of the second rebuff, the Daemon of Hatred thought he would try to influence Santa Claus. So the next day he entered the busy workshop and said:

"Good morning, Santa! I have bad news for you."

"Then run away, like a good fellow," answered Santa Claus. "Bad news is something that should be kept secret and never told."

"You cannot escape this, however," declared the Daemon; "for in the world are a good many who do not believe in Santa Claus, and these you are bound to hate bitterly, since they have so wronged you."

"Stuff and rubbish!" cried Santa.

"And there are others who resent your making children happy and who sneer at you and call you a foolish old rattlepate! You are quite right to hate such base slanderers, and you ought to be revenged upon them for their evil words."

"But I *don't* hate 'em!" exclaimed Santa Claus positively. "Such people do me no real harm, but merely render themselves and their children unhappy. Poor things! I'd much rather help them any day than injure them."

Indeed, the Daemons could not tempt old Santa Claus in any way. On the contrary, he was shrewd enough to see that their object in visiting him was to make mischief and trouble, and his cheery laughter disconcerted the evil ones and showed to them the folly of such an undertaking. So they abandoned honeyed words and determined to use force.

It was well known that no harm can come to Santa Claus while he is in the Laughing Valley, for the Fairies, and Ryls, and Knooks all protect him. But on Christmas Eve he drives his reindeer out into the big world, carrying a sleigh-load of toys and pretty gifts to the children; and this was the time and the occasion when his enemies had the best chance to injure him.

So the Daemons laid their plans and awaited the arrival of Christmas Eve.

The moon shone big and white in the sky, and the snow lay crisp and sparkling on the ground as Santa Claus cracked his whip and sped away out of the Valley into the great world beyond. The roomy sleigh was packed full with huge sacks of toys, and as the reindeer dashed onward our jolly old Santa laughed and whistled and sang for very joy. For in all his merry life this was the one day in the year when he was happiest—the day he lovingly bestowed the treasures of his workshop upon the little children.

BEFORE HE COULD RESIST OR CRY OUT, SANTA WAS JARRED FROM THE SEAT OF THE SLEIGH AND TUMBLED INTO A SNOWBANK.

It would be a busy night for him, he well knew. As he whistled and shouted and cracked his whip again, he reviewed in mind all the towns and cities and farm-houses where he was expected, and figured that he had just enough presents to go around and make every child happy. The reindeer knew exactly what was expected of them, and dashed along so swiftly that their feet scarcely seemed to touch the snow-covered ground.

Suddenly a strange thing happened: a rope shot through the moonlight and a big noose that was in the end of it settled over the arms and body of Santa Claus and drew tight. Before he could resist or even cry out, he was jerked from the seat of the sleigh and tumbled head foremost into a snowbank, while the reindeer rushed onward with the load of toys and carried it quickly out of sight and sound.

"HA, HA," LAUGHED THE DAEMONS, RUBBING THEIR HANDS TOGETHER WITH CRUEL GLEE; "WHAT WILL THE CHILDREN DO NOW?"

Such a surprising experience confused old Santa for a moment, and when he had collected his senses he found that the wicked Daemons had pulled him from the snow-drift and bound him tightly with many coils of the stout rope. And then they carried the kidnapped Santa Claus away to their mountain, where they thrust the prisoner into a secret cave and chained him to the rocky wall so that he could not escape.

"Ha, ha!" laughed the Daemons, rubbing their hands together with cruel glee. "What will the children do now? How they will cry and scold and storm when they find there are no toys in their stockings and no gifts on their Christmas trees! And what a lot of punishment they will receive from their parents, and how they will flock to our Caves of Selfishness, and Envy, and Hatred, and Malice! We have done a mighty clever thing, we Daemons of the Caves!"

NOW IT SO CHANCED THAT on this Christmas Eve the good Santa Claus had taken with him in his sleigh Nuter the Ryl, Peter the Knook, Kilter the Pixie, and a small fairy named Wisk—his four favorite assistants. These little people he had often found very useful in helping him to distribute his gifts to the children, and when their master was so suddenly dragged from the sleigh they were all snugly tucked underneath the seat, where the sharp wind could not reach them.

The tiny immortals knew nothing of the capture of Santa Claus until some time after he had disappeared. But finally they missed his cheery voice, and as their master always sang or whistled on his journeys, the silence warned them that something was wrong.

Little Wisk stuck out his head from underneath the seat and found Santa Claus gone and no one to direct the flight of the reindeer.

"Whoa!" he called out, and the deer obediently slackened speed and came to a halt.

Peter and Nuter and Kilter all jumped upon the seat and looked back over the track made by the sleigh. But Santa Claus had been left miles and miles behind.

"What shall we do?" asked Wisk anxiously, all the mirth and mischief banished from his wee face by this great calamity.

"We must go back at once and find our master," said Nuter the Ryl, who thought and spoke with much deliberation.

"No, no!" exclaimed Peter the Knook, who, cross and

crabbed though he was, might always be depended upon in an emergency. "If we delay, or go back, there will not be time to get the toys to the children before morning; and that would grieve Santa Claus more than anything else."

"It is certain that some wicked creatures have captured him," added Kilter, thoughtfully; "and their object must be to make the children unhappy. So our first duty is to get the toys distributed as carefully as if Santa Claus were himself present. Afterward we can search for our master and easily secure his freedom."

This seemed such good and sensible advice that the others at once resolved to adopt it. So Peter the Knook called to the reindeer, and the faithful animals again sprang forward and dashed over hill and valley, through forest and plain, until they came to the houses wherein children lay sleeping and dreaming of the pretty gifts they would find on Christmas morning.

The little immortals had set themselves a difficult task; for although they had assisted Santa Claus on many of his journeys, their master had always directed and guided them and told them exactly what he wished them to do. But now they had to distribute the toys according to their own judgment, and they did not understand children as well as did old Santa. So it is no wonder they made some laughable errors.

Mamie Brown, who wanted a doll, got a drum instead; and a drum is of no use to a girl who loves dolls. And Charlie Smith, who delights to romp and play out of doors, and who wanted some new rubber boots to keep his feet dry, received a sewing-box filled with colored worsteds and threads and needles, which made him so provoked that he thoughtlessly called our dear Santa Claus a fraud.

Had there been many such mistakes the Daemons would have accomplished their evil purpose and made the children unhappy. But the little friends of the absent Santa Claus labored faithfully and intelligently to carry out their master's ideas, and they made fewer errors than might be expected under such unusual circumstances.

And, although they worked as swiftly as possible, day had begun to break before the toys and other presents were all distributed; so for the first time in many years the reindeer trotted into the Laughing Valley, on their return, in broad daylight, with the brilliant sun peeping over the edge of the Forest to prove they were far behind their accustomed hours.

Having put the deer in the stable, the little folk began to wonder how they might rescue their master; and they realized they must discover, first of all, what had happened to him and where he was.

So Wisk the Fairy transported himself to the bower of the Fairy Queen, which was located deep in the heart of the Forest of Burzee; and once there, it did not take him long to find out all about the naughty Daemons and how they had kidnapped the good Santa Claus to prevent his making children happy. The Fairy Queen also promised her assistance, and then, fortified by this powerful support, Wisk flew back to where Nuter and Peter and Kilter awaited him, and the four counseled together and laid plans to rescue their master from his enemies.

IT IS possible that Santa Claus was not as merry as usual during the night that succeeded his capture. For although he had faith in the judgment of his little friends he could not avoid a certain amount of worry, and an anxious look would creep at times into his kind old eyes as he thought of the disappointment that might await his dear little children. And the Daemons, who guarded him by turns, one after another, did not neglect to taunt him with contemptuous words in his helpless condition.

When Christmas Day dawned the Daemon of Malice was guarding the prisoner, and his tongue was sharper than that of any of the others.

"The children are waking up, Santa!" he cried. "They are waking up to find their stockings empty! Ho, ho! How they will quarrel, and wail, and stamp their feet in anger! Our caves will be full to-day, old Santa! Our caves are sure to be full!"

But to this, as to other like taunts, Santa Claus answered nothing. He was much grieved by his capture, it is true; but his courage did not forsake him. And, finding that the prisoner would not reply to his jeers, the Daemon of Malice presently went away, and sent the Daemon of Repentance to take his place.

This last personage was not so disagreeable as the others. He had gentle and refined features, and his voice was soft and pleasant in tone.

"My brother Daemons do not trust me overmuch," said he, as he entered the cavern; "but it is morning, now, and the mischief is done. You cannot visit the children again for another year."

"That is true," answered Santa Claus, almost cheerfully; "Christmas Eve is past, and for the first time in centuries I have not visited my children."

"The little ones will be greatly disappointed," murmured the Daemon of Repentance, almost regretfully; "but that cannot be helped now. Their grief is likely to make the children selfish and envious and hateful, and if they come to the Caves of the Daemons to-day I shall get a chance to lead some of them to my Cave of Repentance."

"Do you never repent, yourself?" asked Santa Claus, curiously.

"Oh, yes, indeed," answered the Daemon. "I am even now repenting that I assisted in your capture. Of course it is too late to remedy the evil that has been done; but repentance, you know, can come only after an evil thought or deed, for in the beginning there is nothing to repent of."

"So I understand," said Santa Claus. "Those who avoid evil need never visit your cave."

"As a rule, that is true," replied the Daemon; "yet you, who have done no evil, are about to visit my cave at once; for to prove that I sincerely regret my share in your capture I am going to permit you to escape."

WITH THIS HE OPENED A BACK DOOR THAT LET IN A FLOOD OF SUNSHINE.

This speech greatly surprised the prisoner, until he reflected that it was just what might be expected of the Daemon of Repentance. The fellow at once busied himself untying the knots that bound Santa Claus and unlocking the chains that fastened him to the wall. Then he led the way through a long tunnel until they both emerged in the Cave of Repentance.

"I hope you will forgive me," said the Daemon pleadingly. "I am not really a bad person, you know; and I believe I accomplish a great deal of good in the world."

With this he opened a back door that let in a flood of sunshine, and Santa Claus sniffed the fresh air gratefully.

"I bear no malice," said he to the Daemon, in a gentle voice; "and I am sure the world would be a dreary place without you. So, good morning, and a Merry Christmas to you!"

With these words he stepped out to greet the bright morning, and a moment later he was trudging along, whistling softly to himself, on his way to his home in the Laughing Valley.

Marching over the snow toward the mountain was a vast army, made up of the most curious creatures imaginable. There were numberless Knooks from the Forest, as rough and crooked in appearance as the gnarled branches of the trees they ministered to. And there were dainty Ryls from the fields, each one bearing the emblem of the flower or plant it guarded. Behind these were many ranks of Pixies, Gnomes and Nymphs, and in the rear a thousand beautiful Fairies floated along in gorgeous array.

This wonderful army was led by Wisk, Peter, Nuter and Kilter, who had assembled it to rescue Santa Claus from captivity and to punish the Daemons who had dared to take him away from his beloved children.

And, although they looked so bright and peaceful, the little immortals were armed with powers that would be very terrible to those who had incurred their anger. Woe to the Daemons of the Caves if this mighty army of vengeance ever met them!

But lo! coming to meet his loyal friends appeared the imposing form of Santa Claus, his white beard floating in the breeze and his bright eyes sparkling with pleasure at this proof of the love and veneration he had inspired in the hearts of the most powerful creatures in existence.

And while they clustered around him and danced with glee at his safe return, he gave them earnest thanks for their support. But Wisk, and Nuter, and Peter, and Kilter, he embraced affectionately.

BUT LO! COMING TO MEET HIS LOYAL FRIENDS APPEARED THE
IMPOSING FORM OF SANTA CLAUS, HIS BRIGHT EYES
SPARKLING WITH PLEASURE.

"It is useless to pursue the Daemons," said Santa Claus to the army. "They have their place in the world, and can never be destroyed. But that is a great pity, nevertheless," he continued, musingly.

So the Fairies, and Knooks, and Pixies, and Ryls all escorted the good man to his castle, and there left him to talk over the events of the night with his little assistants.

Wisk had already rendered himself invisible and flown through the big world to see how the children were getting along on this bright Christmas morning; and by the time he returned, Peter had finished telling Santa Claus of how they had distributed the toys.

"We really did very well," cried the Fairy, in a pleased voice; "for I found little unhappiness among the children this morning. Still, you must not get captured again, my dear master; for we might not be so fortunate another time in carrying out your ideas."

He then related the mistakes that had been made, and which he had not discovered until his tour of inspection. And

Santa Claus at once sent him with rubber boots for Charlie Smith, and a doll for Mamie Brown; so that even those two disappointed ones became happy.

As for the wicked Daemons of the Caves, they were filled with anger and chagrin when they found that their clever capture of Santa Claus had come to naught. Indeed, no one on that Christmas Day appeared to be at all selfish, or envious, or hateful. And, realizing that while the children's saint had so many powerful friends it was folly to oppose him, the Daemons never again attempted to interfere with his journeys on Christmas Eve.

(EXCERPT FROM) THE ROAD TO OZ

ILLUSTRATED BY JOHN R. NEILL

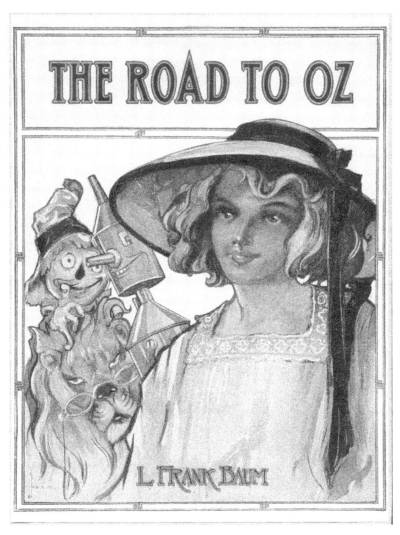

The Road to Oz *original dust jacket, 1909. The dust jacket design differed from the book cover design.*

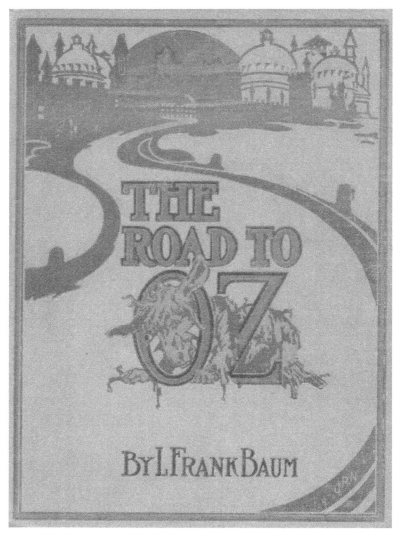

The Road to Oz *original cover, 1909.*

THE ROYAL HISTORIAN of Oz summarized The Road to Oz *as such: "We like to think of this volume as 'The Party Book of Oz.' Almost everyone loves a party, and when Ozma has a birthday party with notables from every part of Fairyland attending—well! It is just like attending Ozma's party in person. You meet the famous of Oz, and lots of others, such as Queen Zixi of Ix, John Dough, Chick the Cherub, the Queen of Merryland, Para Bruin the rubber bear and— best of all—Santa Claus himself! Of course there are lots of adventures on that famous road to Oz before the party, during which Dorothy, on her way to Oz for the fourth time, meets such heartwarming characters as the Shaggy Man, Button-Bright, and lovely Polychrome, daughter of the rainbow."*

"TO MY READERS: Well, my dears, here is what you have asked for: another 'Oz Book' about Dorothy's strange adventures. Toto is in this story, because you wanted him to be there, and many other characters which you will recognize are in the story, too. Indeed, the wishes of my little correspondents have been considered as carefully as possible, and if the story is not exactly as you would have written it yourselves, you must remember that a story has to be a story before it can be written down, and the writer cannot change it much without spoiling it.

"In the preface to 'Dorothy and the Wizard in Oz' I said I would like to write some stories that were not 'Oz' stories, because I thought I had written about Oz long enough; but since that volume was published I have been fairly deluged with letters from children imploring me to 'write more about Dorothy,' and 'more about Oz,' and since I write only to please the children I shall try to respect their wishes.

"There are some new characters in this book that ought to win your love. I'm very fond of the shaggy man myself, and I think you will like him, too. As for Polychrome—the Rainbow's Daughter— and stupid little Button-Bright, they seem to have brought a new element of fun into these Oz stories, and I am glad I discovered them. Yet I am anxious to have you write and tell me how you like them.

"Since this book was written I have received some very remark- able news from The Land of Oz, which has greatly astonished me. I believe it will astonish you, too, my dears, when you hear it. But it is such a long and exciting story that it must be saved for another book —and perhaps that book will be the last story that will ever be told about The Land of Oz."

L. Frank Baum
Coronado, 1909
From the original preface to The Road to Oz

Editor's note: The Road to Oz *was Baum's fifth Oz book, bringing Dorothy and Toto, along with a few friends, back to Oz in time for Princess Ozma's birthday celebration. Here, we pick up the story in time for the last three chapters, just as Santa arrives for the big party.*

To the extent possible, the text of this story, to include spellings such as "good-bye" and "every one," is left as Baum originally wrote it.

THE ROAD TO OZ

BY

L. FRANK BAUM

AUTHOR OF THE LAND OF OZ, OZMA OF OZ, DOROTHY
AND THE WIZARD IN OZ, ETC.

ILLUSTRATED BY

JOHN R. NEILL

Important Arrivals

First entered a band of Ryls from the Happy Valley, all merry little sprites like fairy elves. A dozen crooked Knooks followed from the great Forest of Burzee. They had long whiskers and pointed caps and curling toes, yet were no taller than Button-Bright's shoulder. With this group came a man so easy to recognize and so important and dearly beloved throughout the known world, that all present rose to their feet and bowed their heads in respectful homage, even before the High Chamberlain knelt to announce his name.

"The most Mighty and Loyal Friend of Children, His Supreme Highness—Santa Claus!" said the Chamberlain, in an awed voice.

"Well, well, well! Glad to see you—glad to meet you all!" cried Santa Claus, briskly, as he trotted up the long room.

He was round as an apple, with a fresh rosy face, laughing eyes, and a bushy beard as white as snow. A red cloak trimmed with beautiful ermine hung from his shoulders and upon his back was a basket filled with pretty presents for the Princess Ozma.

"Hello, Dorothy; still having adventures?" he asked in his jolly way, as he took the girl's hand in both his own.

"How did you know my name, Santa?" she replied, feeling more shy in the presence of this immortal saint than she ever had before in her young life.

"Why, don't I see you every Christmas Eve, when you're asleep?" he rejoined, pinching her blushing cheek.

"Oh; do you?"

"And here's Button-Bright, I declare!" cried Santa Claus, holding up the boy to kiss him. "What a long way from home you are; dear me!"

"Do you know Button-Bright, too?" questioned Dorothy, eagerly.

"Indeed I do. I've visited his home several Christmas Eves."

"And do you know his father?" asked the girl.

"Certainly, my dear. Who else do you suppose brings him his Christmas neckties and stockings?" with a sly wink at the Wizard.

"Then where does he live? We're just crazy to know, 'cause Button-Bright's lost," she said.

Santa laughed and laid his finger aside of his nose as if thinking what to reply. He leaned over and whispered something in the Wizard's ear, at which the Wizard smiled and nodded as if he understood.

Now Santa Claus spied Polychrome, and trotted over to where she stood.

"Seems to me the Rainbow's Daughter is farther from home than any of you," he observed, looking at the pretty maiden admiringly. "I'll have to tell your father where you are, Polly, and send him to get you."

"Please do, dear Santa Claus," implored the little maid, beseechingly.

"But just now we must all have a jolly good time at Ozma's party," said the old gentleman, turning to put his presents on the table with the others already there. "It isn't often I find time to leave my castle, as you know; but Ozma invited me and I just couldn't help coming to celebrate the happy occasion."

MERRY RYLS AND CROOKED KNOOKS

"I'm so glad!" exclaimed Dorothy.

"These are my Ryls," pointing to the little sprites squatting around him. "Their business is to paint the colors of the flowers when they bud and bloom; but I brought the merry fellows along to see Oz, and they've left their paint-pots behind them. Also I brought these crooked Knooks, whom I love. My dears, the Knooks are much nicer than they look, for their duty is to water and care for the young trees of the Forest, and they do their work faithfully and well. It's hard work, though, and it makes my Knooks crooked and gnarled, like the trees them-selves; but their hearts are big and kind, as are the hearts of all who do good in our beautiful world."

"I've read of the Ryls and Knooks," said Dorothy, looking upon these little workers with interest.

Santa Claus turned to talk with the Scarecrow and the Tin Woodman, and he also said a kind word to the Shaggy Man, and afterward went away to ride the Saw-Horse around the Emerald City. "For," said he, "I must see all the grand sights while I am here and have the chance, and Ozma has promised to let me ride the Saw-Horse because I'm getting fat and short of breath."

"Where are your reindeer?" asked Polychrome.

"I left them at home, for it is too warm for them in this sunny country," he answered. "They're used to winter weather when they travel."

In a flash he was gone, and the Ryls and Knooks with him; but they could all hear the golden hoofs of the Saw-Horse ringing on the marble pavement outside, as he pranced away with his noble rider.

Presently the band played again, and the High Chamber-lain announced:

"Her Gracious Majesty, the Queen of Merryland."

They looked earnestly to discover whom this queen might be, and saw advancing up the room an exquisite wax doll, dressed in dainty fluffs and ruffles and spangled gown. She was almost as big as Button-Bright, and her cheeks and mouth and eyebrow were prettily painted in delicate colors. Her blue eyes stared a bit, being of glass, yet the expression upon her Majesty's face was quite pleasant and decidedly winning. With the Queen of Merryland were four wooden soldiers, two stalking ahead of her with much dignity and two following behind, like a royal bodyguard. The soldiers were painted in bright colors and carried wooden guns, and after them came a fat little man who attracted attention at once, although he seemed modest and retiring. For he was made of candy, and carried a tin sugar-sifter filled with powdered sugar, with which he dusted himself frequently so that he wouldn't stick to things if he touched them. The High Chamberlain had called him "The Candy Man of Merryland," and Dorothy saw that one of his thumbs looked as if it had been bitten off by someone who was fond of candy and couldn't resist the temptation.

The wax doll Queen spoke prettily to Dorothy and the others, and sent her loving greetings to Ozma before she retired to the rooms prepared for her. She had brought a birthday present wrapped in tissue paper and tied with pink and blue ribbons, and one of the wooden soldiers placed it on the table with the other gifts. But the Candy Man did not go to his room, because he said he preferred to stay and talk with the Scare-crow and Tik-Tok and the Wizard and Tin Woodman, whom he declared the queerest people he had ever met. Button-Bright was glad the Candy Man stayed in the Throne-Room, because the boy thought this guest smelled deliciously of wintergreen and maple sugar.

The Braided Man now entered the room, having been fortunate enough to receive an invitation to the Princess Ozma's party. He was from a cave halfway between the Invisible Valley and the Country of the Gargoyles, and his hair and whiskers were so long that he was obliged to plait them into many braids that hung to his feet, and every braid was tied with a bow of colored ribbon.

"I've brought Princess Ozma a box of flutters for her birthday," said the Braided Man, earnestly; "and I hope she will like them, for they are the finest quality I have ever made."

"I'm sure she will be greatly pleased," said Dorothy, who remembered the Braided Man well; and the Wizard introduced the guest to the rest of the company and made him sit down in a chair and keep quiet, for, if allowed, he would talk continually about his flutters.

The band then played a welcome to another set of guests, and into the Throne-Room swept the handsome and stately Queen of Ev. Beside her was young King Evardo, and following them came the entire royal family of five Princesses and four Princes of Ev. The Kingdom of Ev lay just across the Deadly Desert to the North of Oz, and once Ozma and her people had rescued the Queen of Ev and her ten children from the Nome King, who had enslaved them. Dorothy had been present on this adventure, so she greeted the royal family cordially; and all the visitors were delighted to meet the little Kansas girl again. They knew Tik-Tok and Billina, too, and the Scarecrow and Tin Woodman, as well as the Lion and Tiger; so there was a joyful reunion, as you may imagine, and it was fully an hour before the Queen and her train retired to their rooms. Perhaps they would not have gone then had not the band begun to play to announce new arrivals; but before they left the great Throne-Room King Evardo added to Ozma's birthday presents a diadem of diamonds set in radium.

The next comer proved to be King Renard of Foxville; or King Dox, as he preferred to be called. He was magnificently dressed in a new feather costume and wore white kid mittens over his paws and a flower in his button-hole and had his hair parted in the middle.

HER MAJESTY, QUEEN ZIXI OF IX

King Dox thanked Dorothy fervently for getting him the invitation to come to Oz, which he had all his life longed to visit. He strutted around rather absurdly as he was introduced to all the famous people assembled in the Throne-Room, and when he learned that Dorothy was a Princess of Oz the Fox King insisted on kneeling at her feet and afterward retired backward—a dangerous thing to do, as he might have stubbed his paw and tumbled over.

No sooner was he gone than the blasts of bugles and clatter of drums and cymbals announced important visitors, and the High Chamberlain assumed his most dignified tone as he threw open the door and said proudly:

"Her Sublime and Resplendent Majesty, Queen Zixi of Ix! His Serene and Tremendous Majesty, King Bud of Noland. Her Royal Highness, the Princess Fluff."

That three such high and mighty royal personages should arrive at once was enough to make Dorothy and her companions grow solemn and assume their best company manners; but when the exquisite beauty of Queen Zixi met their eyes they thought they had never beheld anything so charming. Dorothy decided that Zixi must be about sixteen years old, but the Wizard whispered to her that this wonderful queen had lived thousands of years, but knew the secret of remaining always fresh and beautiful.

King Bud of Noland and his dainty fair-haired sister, the Princess Fluff, were friends of Zixi, as their kingdoms were adjoining, so they had traveled together from their far-off domains to do honor to Ozma of Oz on the occasion of her birthday. They brought many splendid gifts; so the table was now fairly loaded down with presents.

Dorothy and Polly loved the Princess Fluff the moment they saw her, and little King Bud was so frank and boyish that Button-Bright accepted him as a chum at once and did not want him to go away. But it was after noon now, and the royal guests must prepare their toilets for the grand banquet at which they were to assemble that evening to meet the reigning Princess of this Fairyland; so Queen Zixi was shown to her room by a troop of maidens led by Jellia Jamb, and Bud and Fluff presently withdrew to their own apartments.

"My! what a big party Ozma is going to have," exclaimed Dorothy. "I guess the palace will be chock full, Button-Bright; don't you think so?"

"Don't know," said the boy.

"But we must go to our rooms, pretty soon, to dress for the banquet," continued the girl.

"I don't have to dress," said the Candy Man from Merry-land. "All I need do is to dust myself with fresh sugar."

"Tik-Tok and I always wear the same suits of clothes," said the Tin Woodman; "and so does our friend the Scarecrow."

"My feathers are good enough for any occasion," cried Billina, from her corner.

"Then I shall leave you four to welcome any new guests that come," said Dorothy; "for Button-Bright and I must look our very best at Ozma's banquet."

"Who is still to come?" asked the Scarecrow.

"Well, there's King Kika-bray of Dunkiton, and Johnny

Dooit, and the Good Witch of the North. But Johnny Dooit may not get here until late, he's so very busy."

"We will receive them and give them a proper welcome," promised the Scarecrow. "So run along, little Dorothy, and get yourself dressed."

The Grand Banquet

I WISH I could tell you how fine the company was that assembled that evening at Ozma's royal banquet. A long table was spread in the center of the great dining-hall of the palace and the splendor of the decorations and the blaze of lights and jewels was acknowledged to be the most magnificent sight that any of the guests had ever seen.

The jolliest person present, as well as the most important, was of course, old Santa Claus; so he was given the seat of honor at one end of the table while at the other end sat Princess Ozma, the hostess.

John Dough, Queen Zixi, King Bud, the Queen of Ev and her son Evardo, and the Queen of Merryland had golden thrones to sit in, while the others were supplied with beautiful chairs.

At the upper end of the banquet room was a separate table provided for the animals. Toto sat at one end of this table, with a bib tied around his neck and a silver platter to eat from. At the other end was placed a small stand, with a low rail around the edge of it, for Billina and her chicks. The rail kept the ten little Dorothys from falling off the stand, while the Yellow Hen could easily reach over and take her food from her tray upon the table. At other places sat the Hungry Tiger, the Cowardly Lion, the Saw-Horse, the Rubber Bear, the Fox King and the Donkey King; they made quite a company of animals.

At the lower end of the great room was another table, at which sat the Ryls and Knooks who had come with Santa Claus, the wooden soldiers who had come with the Queen of Merryland, and the Hilanders and Lolanders who had come with John Dough. Here were also seated the officers of the royal palace and of Ozma's army.

The splendid costumes of those at the three tables made a gorgeous and glittering display that no one present was ever likely to forget; perhaps there has never been in any part of the world at any time another assemblage of such wonderful people as that which gathered this evening to honor the birthday of the Ruler of Oz.

When all the members of the company were in their places an orchestra of five hundred pieces, in a balcony overlooking the banquet room, began to play sweet and delightful music. Then a door draped with royal green opened, and in came the fair and girlish Princess Ozma, who now greeted her guests in person for the first time.

As she stood by her throne at the head of the banquet table every eye was turned eagerly upon the lovely Princess, who was as dignified as she was bewitching, and who smiled upon all her old and new friends in a way that touched their hearts and brought an answering smile to every face.

Each guest had been served with a crystal goblet filled with lacasa, which is a sort of nectar famous in Oz and nicer to drink than soda-water or lemonade. Santa now made a pretty speech in verse, congratulating Ozma on having a birthday, and asking every one present to drink to the health and happiness of their dearly beloved hostess. This was done with great enthusiasm by those who were made so they could drink at all, and those who could not drink politely touched the rims of their goblets to their lips. All seated themselves at the tables and the servants of the Princess began serving the feast.

I am quite sure that only in Fairyland could such a delicious repast be prepared. The dishes were of precious metals set with brilliant jewels and the good things to eat which were placed upon them were countless in number and of exquisite flavor. Several present, such as the Candy Man, the Rubber Bear, Tik-Tok, and the Scarecrow, were not made so they could eat, and the Queen of Merryland contented herself with a small dish of sawdust; but these enjoyed the pomp and glitter of the gorgeous scene as much as did those who feasted.

DRINKING THE HEALTH OF PRINCESS OZMA OF OZ

The Woggle-Bug read his "Ode to Ozma," which was written in very good rhythm and was well received by the company. The Wizard added to the entertainment by making a big pie appear before Dorothy, and when the little girl cut the pie the nine tiny piglets leaped out of it and danced around the table, while the orchestra played a merry tune. This amused the company very much, but they were even more pleased when Polychrome, whose hunger had been easily satisfied, rose from the table and performed her graceful and bewildering Rainbow Dance for them. When it was ended the people clapped their hands and the animals clapped their paws, while Billina cackled and the Donkey King brayed approval.

Johnny Dooit was present, and of course he proved he could do wonders in the way of eating, as well as in everything else that he undertook to do; the Tin Woodman sang a love song, every one joining in the chorus; and the wooden soldiers from Merryland gave an exhibition of a lightning drill with their wooden muskets; the Ryls and Knooks danced the Fairy Circle; and the Rubber Bear bounced himself all around the room. There was laughter and merriment on every side, and everybody was having a royal good time. Button-Bright was so excited and interested that he paid little attention to his fine dinner and a great deal of attention to his queer companions; and perhaps he was wise to do this, because he could eat at any other time.

The feasting and merrymaking continued until late in the evening, when they separated to meet again the next morning and take part in the birthday celebration, to which this royal banquet was merely the introduction.

The Birthday Celebration

A CLEAR, perfect day, with a gentle breeze and a sunny sky, greeted Princess Ozma as she wakened next morning, the anniversary of her birth. While it was yet early all the city was astir and crowds of people came from all parts of the Land of Oz to witness the festivities in honor of their girl Ruler's birthday.

The noted visitors from foreign countries, who had all been transported to the Emerald City by means of the Magic Belt, were as much a show to the Ozites as were their own familiar celebrities, and the streets leading from the royal palace to the jeweled gates were thronged with men, women, and children to see the procession as it passed out to the green fields where the ceremonies were to take place.

And what a great procession it was!

First came a thousand young girls—the prettiest in the land —dressed in white muslin, with green sashes and hair ribbons, bearing great baskets of red roses. As they walked they scattered these flowers upon the marble pavements, so that the way was carpeted thick with roses for the procession to walk upon.

Then came the Rulers of the four Kingdoms of Oz; the Emperor of the Winkies, the Monarch of the Munchkins, the King of the Quadlings and the Sovereign of the Gillikins, each wearing a long chain of emeralds around his neck to show that he was a vassal of the Ruler of the Emerald City.

Next marched the Emerald City Cornet Band, clothed in green-and-gold uniforms and playing the "Ozma Two-Step." The Royal Army of Oz followed, consisting of twenty-seven officers, from the Captain-General down to the Lieutenants. There were no privates in Ozma's Army because soldiers were not needed to fight battles, but only to look important, and an officer always looks more imposing than a private.

While the people cheered and waved their hats and handkerchiefs, there came walking the Royal Princess Ozma, looking so pretty and sweet that it is no wonder her people love her so dearly. She had decided she would not ride in her chariot that day, as she preferred to walk in the procession with her favored subjects and her guests. Just in front of her trotted the living Blue Bear Rug owned by old Dyna, which wobbled clumsily on its four feet because there was nothing but the skin to support them, with a stuffed head at one end and a stubby tail at the other. But whenever Ozma paused in her walk the Bear Rug would flop down flat upon the ground for the princess to stand upon until she resumed her progress.

Following the Princess stalked her two enormous beasts, the Cowardly Lion and the Hungry Tiger, and even if the Army had not been there these two would have been powerful enough to guard their mistress from any harm.

Next marched the invited guests, who were loudly cheered by the people of Oz along the road, and were therefore obliged to bow to right and left almost every step of the way. First was Santa Claus, who, because he was fat and not used to walking, rode the wonderful Saw-Horse. The merry old gentleman had a basket of small toys with him, and he tossed the toys one by one to the children as he passed by. His Ryls and Knooks marched close behind him.

Queen Zixi of Ix came after; then John Dough and the Cherub, with the rubber bear named Para Bruin strutting between them on its hind legs; then the Queen of Merryland, escorted by her wooden soldiers; then King Bud of Noland and his sister, the Princess Fluff; then the Queen of Ev and her ten royal children; then the Braided Man and the Candy Man, side by side; then King Dox of Foxville and King Kik-a-bray of Dunkiton, who by this time had become good friends; and finally Johnny Dooit, in his leather apron, smoking his long pipe.

These wonderful personages were not more heartily cheered by the people than were those who followed after them in the procession. Dorothy was a general favorite, and she walked arm in arm with the Scarecrow, who was beloved by all. Then came Polychrome and Button-Bright, and the people loved the Rainbow's pretty Daughter and the beautiful blue-eyed boy as soon as they saw them. The Shaggy Man in his shaggy new suit attracted much attention because he was such a novelty. With regular steps tramped the machine-man Tik-Tok, and there was more cheering when the Wizard of Oz followed in the procession. The Woggle-Bug and Jack Pump-kinhead were next, and behind them Glinda the Sorceress and the Good Witch of the North. Finally came Billina, with her brood of chickens to whom she clucked anxiously to keep them together and to hasten them along so they would not delay the procession.

Another band followed, this time the Tin Band of the Emperor of the Winkies, playing a beautiful march called, "There's No Plate Like Tin." Then came the servants of the Royal Palace, in a long line, and behind them all the people joined the procession and marched away through the emerald gates and out upon the broad green.

Here had been erected a splendid pavilion, with a grand-stand big enough to seat all the royal party and those who had taken part in the procession. Over the pavilion, which was of green silk and cloth of gold, countless banners waved in the breeze. Just in front of this, and connected with it by a runway, had been built a broad platform, so that all the spectators could see plainly the entertainment provided for them.

The Wizard now became Master of Ceremonies, as Ozma had placed the conduct of the performance in his hands. After the people had all congregated about the platform and the royal party and the visitors were seated in the grandstand, the Wizard skillfully performed some feats of juggling glass balls and lighted candles. He tossed a dozen or so of them high in the air and caught them one by one as they came down, without missing any.

Then he introduced the Scarecrow, who did a sword-swal-lowing act that aroused much interest. After this the Tin

Woodman gave an exhibition of Swinging the Axe, which he made to whirl around him so rapidly that the eye could scarcely follow the motion of the gleaming blade. Glinda the Sorceress then stepped upon the platform, and by her magic made a big tree grow in the middle of the space, made blossoms appear upon the tree, and made the blossoms become delicious fruit called tamornas; and so great was the quantity of fruit thus produced that when the servants climbed the tree and tossed it down to the crowd, there was enough to satisfy every person present.

Para Bruin, the rubber bear, climbed to a limb of the big tree, rolled himself into a ball, and dropped to the platform, whence he bounded up again to the limb. He repeated this bouncing act several times, to the great delight of all the children present. After he had finished, and bowed, and returned to his seat, Glinda waved her wand and the tree disappeared; but its fruit still remained to be eaten.

The Good Witch of the North amused the people by transforming ten stones into ten birds, the ten birds into ten lambs, and the ten lambs into ten little girls, who gave a pretty dance and were then transformed into ten stones again, just as they were in the beginning.

Johnny Dooit next came on the platform with his tool-chest, and in a few minutes built a great flying machine; then put his chest in the machine and the whole thing flew away together—Johnny and all—after he had bid good-bye to those present and thanked the Princess for her hospitality.

The Wizard then announced the last act of all, which was considered really wonderful. He had invented a machine to blow huge soap-bubbles, as big as balloons, and this machine was hidden under the platform so that only the rim of the big clay pipe to produce the bubbles showed above the flooring. The tank of soap-suds, and the air-pumps to inflate the bubbles, were out of sight beneath, so that when the bubbles began to grow upon the floor of the platform it really seemed like magic to the people of Oz, who knew nothing about even the common soap-bubbles that our children blow with a penny clay pipe and a basin of soap-and-water.

The Wizard had invented another thing. Usually soap-bubbles are frail and burst easily, lasting only a few moments as they float in the air; but the Wizard added a sort of glue to his soapsuds, which made his bubbles tough; and, as the glue dried rapidly when exposed to the air, the Wizard's bubbles were strong enough to float for hours without breaking.

He began by blowing—by means of his machinery and air-pumps—several large bubbles which he allowed to float upward into the sky, where the sunshine fell upon them and gave them iridescent hues that were most beautiful. This aroused much wonder and delight, because it was a new amusement to every one present—except perhaps Dorothy and Button-Bright, and even they had never seen such big, strong bubbles before.

The Wizard then blew a bunch of small bubbles and afterward blew a big bubble around them so they were left in the center of it; then he allowed the whole mass of pretty globes to float into the air and disappear in the far distant sky.

"That is really fine!" declared Santa Claus, who loved toys and pretty things. "I think, Mr. Wizard, I shall have you blow a bubble around me; then I can float away home and see the country spread out beneath me as I travel. There isn't a spot on earth that I haven't visited, but I usually go in the night-time, riding behind my swift reindeer. Here is a good chance to observe the country by daylight, while I am riding slowly and at my ease."

"Do you think you will be able to guide the bubble?" asked the Wizard.

"Oh yes; I know enough magic to do that," replied Santa Claus. "You blow the bubble, with me inside of it, and I'll be sure to get home in safety."

"Please send me home in a bubble, too!" begged the Queen of Merryland.

"Very well, madam; you shall try the journey first," politely answered old Santa.

The pretty wax doll bade good-bye to the Princess Ozma and the others, and stood on the platform while the Wizard blew a big soap-bubble around her. When completed he allowed the bubble to float slowly upward, and there could be seen the little Queen of Merryland standing in the middle of it and blowing kisses from her fingers to those below. The bubble took a southerly direction, quickly floating out of sight.

"That's a very nice way to travel," said Princess Fluff. "I'd like to go home in a bubble, too."

So the Wizard blew a big bubble around Princess Fluff, and another around King Bud, her brother, and a third one around Queen Zixi; and soon these three bubbles had mounted into the sky and were floating off in a group in the direction of the kingdom of Noland.

The success of these ventures induced the other guests from foreign lands to undertake bubble journeys, also; so the Wizard put them one by one inside his bubbles, and Santa Claus directed the way they should go, because he knew exactly where everybody lived.

Finally Button-Bright said:

"I want to go home, too."

"Why, so you shall!" cried Santa; "for I'm sure your father and mother will be glad to see you again. Mr. Wizard, please blow a big, fine bubble for Button-Bright to ride in, and I'll agree to send him home to his family as safe as safe can be."

"I'm sorry," said Dorothy with a sigh, for she was fond of her little comrade; "but p'raps it's best for Button-Bright to get home; 'cause his folks must be worrying just dreadful."

She kissed the boy, and Ozma kissed him, too, and all the others waved their hands and said good-bye and wished him a pleasant journey.

"Are you glad to leave us, dear?" asked Dorothy, a little wistfully.

"Don't know," said Button-Bright.

He sat down cross-legged on the platform, with his sailor hat tipped back on his head, and the Wizard blew a beautiful bubble all around him.

A minute later it had mounted into the sky, sailing toward the west, and the last they saw of Button-Bright he was still sitting in the middle of the shining globe and waving his sailor-hat at those below.

"Will you ride in a bubble, or shall I send you and Toto home by means of the Magic Belt?" the Princess asked Dorothy.

"Guess I'll use the Belt," replied the little girl. "I'm sort of 'fraid of those bubbles."

"Bow-wow!" said Toto, approvingly. He loved to bark at the bubbles as they sailed away, but he didn't care to ride in one.

THE WIZARD BLEW A BUBBLE AROUND SANTA CLAUS

Santa Claus decided to go next. He thanked Ozma for her hospitality and wished her many happy returns of the day. Then the Wizard blew a bubble around his chubby little body and smaller bubbles around each of his Ryls and Knooks.

As the kind and generous friend of children mounted into

the air the people all cheered at the top of their voices, for they loved Santa Claus dearly; and the little man heard them through the walls of the bubble and waved his hands in return as he smiled down upon them. The band played bravely while every one watched the bubble until it was completely out of sight.

"How 'bout you, Polly?" Dorothy asked her friend. "Are you 'fraid of bubbles, too?"

"No," answered Polychrome, smiling; "but Santa Claus promised to speak to my father as he passed through the sky. So perhaps I shall get home an easier way."

Indeed, the little maid had scarcely made this speech when a sudden radiance filled the air, and while the people looked on in wonder the end of a gorgeous rainbow slowly settled down upon the platform.

With a glad cry the Rainbow's Daughter sprang from her seat and danced along the curve of the bow, mounting gradually upward, while the folds of her gauzy gown whirled and floated around her like a cloud and blended with the colors of the rainbow itself.

"Good-bye, Ozma! Good-bye, Dorothy!" cried a voice they knew belonged to Polychrome; but now the little maiden's form had melted wholly into the rainbow, and their eyes could no longer see her.

Suddenly the end of the rainbow lifted and its colors slowly faded like mist before a breeze. Dorothy sighed deeply and turned to Ozma.

"I'm sorry to lose Polly," she said; "but I guess she's better off with her father; 'cause even the Land of Oz couldn't be like home to a cloud fairy."

"No, indeed," replied the Princess; "but it has been delightful for us to know Polychrome for a little while, and—who knows?—perhaps we may meet the Rainbow's Daughter again, some day."

"GOOD-BYE, OZMA! GOOD-BYE, DOROTHY!"

The entertainment being now ended, all left the pavilion and formed their gay procession back to the Emerald City again. Of Dorothy's recent traveling companions only Toto and the Shaggy Man remained, and Ozma had decided to allow the latter to live in Oz for a time, at least. If he proved honest and true, she promised to let him live there always, and the Shaggy Man was anxious to earn this reward.

They had a nice quiet dinner together and passed a pleasant evening with the Scarecrow, the Tin Woodman, Tik-Tok, and the Yellow Hen for company.

When Dorothy bade them good-night she kissed them all good-bye at the same time. For Ozma had agreed that while Dorothy slept she and Toto should be transported by means of the Magic Belt to her own little bed in the Kansas farmhouse and the little girl laughed as she thought how astonished Uncle Henry and Aunt Em would be when she came down to breakfast with them next morning.

Quite content to have had so pleasant an adventure, and a little tired by all the day's busy scenes, Dorothy clasped Toto in her arms and lay down upon the pretty white bed in her room in Ozma's royal palace.

Presently she was sound asleep.

THE
END

HOW THE WOGGLEBUG AND HIS FRIENDS VISITED SANTA CLAUS

ILLUSTRATED BY WALT MCDOUGALL

EDITOR'S NOTE: Queer Visitors from the Marvelous Land of Oz *was a weekly comic page running for six months in such newspapers as the* Philadelphia North American, *the* Sunday Boston Herald, *and the* Richmond Times-Dispatch, *from August 1904 to February 1905. The comic filled an entire page of the Sunday paper and consisted of a short story and colorful illustrations by Baum and Walt McDougall, respectively. Many of these comics ended by asking, "What did the Wogglebug say?" Each newspaper that ran the comic then offered prizes to readers who mailed in the correct answer.*

⁂

THE ORIGINAL SUMMER, *1904, newspaper announcement for* Queer Visitors from the Marvelous Land of Oz *series declared (note the various spellings of Wogglebug and Tin Woodman):*

. . .

FROM THE LAND of Oz to the United States. Here they come! The Scarecrow and Tinwoodman, Jack Pumpkinhead, the Woggle Bug, the Animated Sawhorse and the Gump. They are on their first vacation away from the Emerald City and the Land of Oz. They want to romp with the children of the United States. The glad news comes to this newspaper as follows:

Proclamation Extraordinary

To MR. L. FRANK BAUM,
by Royal Appointment Historian to the Land of Oz.

At the request of your Highly Esteemed Writeness, I have issued a Decree permitting my beloved subjects, the Scarecrow, the Tin Woodman, the Woggle-Bug and Jack Pumpkinhead, to visit the United States of America, in order that they may accumulate great store of Wisdom and Experience in your most prosaic Country. They are permitted to take with them the Animated Saw-Horse, and their journey will be made in the Flying Gump. They should arrive upon your Earth Planet within a brief space of Time, and I trust you will accord them a warm Welcome and watch carefully over their Interests.

Given under my Hand and Seal at my Royal Palace in the Emerald City in the Ninth Division of the Second Year of my Reign.

SIGNED, Ozma
Reigning Princess of the Fairy-
land of Oz (Successor to the
Wizard of Oz)

What Did the Woggle Bug Say?

Every reader of The Times-Dispatch will find himself or herself puzzling over this perplexing question after he has read the page in the Magazine Section devoted to the doings of the "Queer Visitors From the Marvelous Land of Oz."

The Woggle Bug, wise man of the party, undertakes to answer all questions for his comrades from Oz. He has to answer one each week. His answer is not printed. The reader is left to discover it. The pictures and descriptive matter make this comparatively easy to the active mind. Both the pictures and the story are guides to the solution of the problem, and the question admits of but one correct answer. The puzzles require only ordinary skill.

TWENTY-FIVE DOLLARS IN PRIZES

To stimulate interest in the visit of the people from the Land of Oz The Times-Dispatch will give Twenty Dollars in cash and five copies of Mr. Baum's interesting book "The Marvelous Land of Oz" each month to those of its readers who send in correct or nearly correct answers to the questions put to the Woggle Bug by his companions.

| Sept. 24. | Use This Coupon Only | No. 24. |

To the WOGGLE BUG EDITOR
THE SUNDAY TIMES-DISPATCH, Richmond, Va.:

The answer to the question asked of the Woggle Bug in the Magazine Section of the paper of SUNDAY, SEPTEMBER 18th, is—

Name ....

Street and Number ....

Town or City ....

State ....

No employe of The Times-Dispatch or member of an employe's family is allowed to enter the contest.

FILL OUT THE ABOVE COUPON. Also the coupon to be found each day in The Times-Dispatch until Saturday, September 24th. This gives you a chance to solve the question suggested in the page to-day, and the same next Sunday and each next week-day, until the end of the month. SAVE YOUR COUPONS, and on the last day of the month send them all to the WOGGLE BUG EDITOR, care of Times-Dispatch, Richmond, Va. This will end the contest for September, and the prizes will be awarded very early in the month of October.

$25.00 IN PRIZES WILL BE GIVEN AS FOLLOWS:

1. For the greatest amount of correct answers $15
2. For the next largest amount of correct answers 5
3. For the third largest amount of correct answers 5
4. For the fourth largest number of correct answers 5
5. For the fifth next largest number of correct answers (books) 5
6. For the sixth to tenth holders of correct answers (a contest) 5

$25

RULES OF THE CONTEST.

The largest number of correct answers wins.

All coupons for any one month will be consecutively numbered and must be pinned in an envelope and sent in at the end of their publication.

Only one answer to the question can be posted to the same question each week.

If more than one individual sends every coupon correctly answered and properly arranged, the first prize would be divided between the winners. Other prizes will be given only in case the number of correct answers were the same instead of whole that prize would be divided.

Contestants need not work their puzzle answer to any coupon issued for any one week. A different answer may be written for each day, but if you are sure you are right, you need, of course, give but one answer for the coupon issued for any one Sunday.

All coupons for any one month must be placed in the same envelope and be in the office of the Times-Dispatch by 12 M. of the 10th day of the following month.

Entry form for Baum and McDougall's Wogglebug contest in the Richmond Times-Dispatch *on Saturday, September 24, 1904.*

A typical entry form for the Wogglebug contest, this one taken from the Richmond-Times Dispatch, *reads in part:*

What Did the Woggle Bug Say?

Every reader of the Times-Dispatch *will find himself or herself puzzling over this perplexing question after he has read the page in the Magazine Section devoted to the doings of the "Queer Visitors From the Marvelous Land of Oz."*
The Woggle Bug, wise man of the party, undertakes to answer all questions for his comrades from Oz. He has to answer one each week. His answer is not printed. The reader is left to discover it. The pictures and descriptive matter make this comparatively easy to the active mind. Both the pictures and the story are guides to the solution of the problem, and the question admits of but one correct answer. The puzzles require only ordinary skill.

TWENTY-FIVE DOLLARS IN PRIZES

To stimulate interest in the visit of the people from the Land of Oz, The Times-Dispatch will give Twenty Dollars in cash and five copies of Mr. Baum's interesting book "The Marvelous Land of Oz" each month to those of its readers who send in correct or nearly correct answers to the questions put to the Woggle Bug by his companions.

FILL OUT THE ABOVE COUPON. Also the coupon to be found each day in The Times-Dispatch until Saturday, September 24th. This gives you six chances to answer the question suggested in the page to-day. Do the same next Sunday, and also on each week-day, until the end of the month. SAVE YOUR COUPONS, and on the last day of the month send them all to the WOGGLE BUG EDITOR...

Illustration by McDougall showing Baum (left) and McDougall as part of the announcement of the Queer Visitors from the Marvelous Land Oz *series*

Here is the story from the December 18, 1904 Sunday comics where the Scarecrow, Tin Woodman, and their friends visit Santa Claus, along with the answer as to what the Wogglebug said.

HOW THE WOGGLEBUG AND HIS
FRIENDS VISITED SANTA CLAUS

"It's nearly Christmas time," said the Scarecrow, yesterday, "and I really think we ought to do something for the children of America who have welcomed us so kindly."

"What can we do?" asked the Tin Woodman.

"Why, it seems that on every Christmas Santa Claus brings the children toys for presents. So it strikes me that we also ought to furnish toys for the little ones, to prove our love for them," returned the Scarecrow.

"But where can we get the toys?" the Wogglebug inquired. "We have no money with which to purchase such things."

"True," acknowledged the Straw Man; "but in Oz we do without money, because when we want a thing we create it by means of the magical arts we are learned in. Let us therefore provide, by means of our magic, the toys we require for the children."

This suggestion being agreed to, they all retired to private rooms, that they might create the toys undisturbed and before long the Tin Woodman came back with an armful of tiny tin men that were exact duplicates of himself. They were all jointed in their legs and arms, and their heads could be made to turn to right or left.

Soon after, the Scarecrow entered the room carrying a lot of rag dolls that were small images of himself. These baby scarecrows were very quaint and amusing, and there was no doubt the children would like them. Then Jack Pumpkinhead brought in a number of small pumpkin heads, made out of paper, but with features exactly resembling Jack himself.

"They're hollow inside," said Jack; "but the children can fill them with candy."

When the Wogglebug entered the room he brought quantities of wee wogglebugs, dressed just like himself, and having their four arms and their legs made of wire and covered with fuzzy worsted. These toys were so comical that all the party laughed when they saw them.

"But our friend the Sawhorse must not be neglected," said

the Scarecrow; so he went away and did a little more magic, and soon returned with a drove of small wooden sawhorses, which had wheels under each of their legs, so that the children could draw them over the floor by means of strings.

"Let us carry them to Santa Claus," suggested the Tin Woodman. "He can take them in his sleigh and distribute them with his other Christmas gifts."

This plan being approved, the entire party mounted aboard the Gump, which flew with them far away to the Laughing Valley where Santa Claus lives. They found the dear old man sitting in an easy chair before his fire and smoking a short pipe. He had finished his yearly labors, and his sleigh was already loaded with packages of toys for the children's Christmas, while the ten reindeer stamped impatiently to be off and away upon their journey.

"You are just in time!" exclaimed Santa Claus, "and I will gladly carry your toys to the little ones."

"We would like every child to have one of them," said the Scarecrow.

"But—good gracious, my friends!" cried bluff old Santa, "you haven't enough for a quarter of the children I shall visit."

This news made the people from Oz very sad and downcast; but, noticing this, the good old man added: "Never mind; I'll make them go as far as I can, and these toys are so pretty that next year I will make a lot of them myself, so that every child may get one for Christmas. But now I must be off, or I shall never get my journey finished by Christmas morning."

So Santa Claus placed the toys in his sleigh and himself mounted the seat. The people of Oz also got into the Gump again, and then Santa said, with a sly wink:

"Let's have a race."

"To be sure," agreed the Scarecrow; "but nothing can go so swiftly as the flight of the Gump."

Santa Claus made no answer in words, but he cracked his long whip, and away shot the reindeer —swift as the wind.

The Gump flew as it had never flown before, but every effort to keep pace with the sleigh of jolly Santa was in vain, and presently the people of Oz looked down through the moonlight and saw a tiny speck far ahead of them, which was their last view of the sleigh-load of toys destined for the children's Christmas.

"We are beaten," remarked the Scarecrow. "But I imagine Santa Claus is a greater magician than any that has ever lived in our Land of Oz."

And the Wogglebug quoted, impressively, these lines:

> "'Around the man who seeks a noble end,
> Not angels, but divinities attend.'

"That," said he, "was written by a famous American poet."
"What was his name?" asked the Scarecrow, curiously.
And the Wogglebug told him.

What did the Wogglebug say?

[Ralph Waldo Emerson]

———

ORIGINAL PUBLICATION INFORMATION

Untitled Christmas poem published as part of *The Shaggy Man of Oz* by Jack Snow, 1949.

"Little Bun Rabbit," published in *Mother Goose in Prose*, 1897.

The Life and Adventures of Santa Claus, published 1902.

"A Kidnapped Santa Claus," published in *The Delineator Magazine*, December 1904.

The Road to Oz, published 1909.

"How the Wogglebug and His Friends Visited Santa Claus," published December 18 1904.

These works are in the Public Domain.

Interior artwork images by

Maxfield Parrish, "Little Bun Rabbit"

Mary Cowles Clark, *The Life and Adventures of Santa Claus*

Frederick Richardson, "A Kidnapped Santa Claus"

John R. Neill, *The Road to Oz*

Walt McDougall, "How the Wogglebug and his Friends Visited Santa Claus"

ABOUT THE AUTHOR AND ILLUSTRATORS

Lyman Frank Baum, known popularly as L. Frank Baum, was an American children's author best known for his Land of Oz series. Born in 1856 in New York, Baum worked variously as a playwright and actor, businessman, and newspaper journalist before finding his greatest success in his forties when he began writing children's stories.

Baum's first book for children was 1897's *Mother Goose in Prose*, a collection of stories based on Mother Goose nursery rhymes. His most famous and enduring work, *The Wonderful Wizard of Oz*, was published in 1900. In his lifetime, Baum authored more than 50 novels and over 80 short stories, many under pseudonyms such as Floyd Akers, Laura Bancroft, Edith Van Dyne, and Schuyler Staunton.

In November of 1882, he married Maud Gage, daughter of suffragist Matilda Gage. A known proponent for women's rights, he often worked his advocacy into his writings, including some of the Oz and Edith Van Dyne stories. Baum died at the age of 62 on May 6, 1919, following a stroke, in Hollywood, California. *Glinda of Oz*, the fourteenth and final book he wrote for the Oz series, was published a year later, in July of 1920.

Maxfield Parrish (1870-1966) studied architecture in the late 1880s and attended the Pennsylvania Academy of Fine Arts from 1892 to 1895. In the mid-1880s, his work began appearing in magazines such as *Harper's Bazaar* and *Scribner's*, and later *Collier's*, *Life*, and *Hearst's*. Many of his works featured fantastical images and landscapes and by 1910 Parrish was so successful he was allegedly earning over $100,000 per year. One of his most well-known works, *Daybreak*, sold for over $7 million in 2006. He illustrated his first book, L. Frank Baum's *Mother Goose in Prose*, in 1897. In 2001 Parrish was honored as part of a US postage stamp series featuring great American illustrators.

Mary Seymour Cowles Clark (1871-1950) studied art at the Art Students League in New York and is believed to have met L. Frank Baum when he was visiting relatives in Syracuse. She created over 150 illustrations, large and small, for Baum's *The Life and Adventures of Santa Claus*. Although she provided drawings for very few other books, she continued as an artist and was known to spend her summers in Siasconset (Nantucket Island) painting, drawing, and crafting needlework.

Frederick Richardson (1862-1937) studied art in St. Louis and in Paris, and later taught at the Chicago Art Institute. Richardson served as an illustrator for the *Chicago Daily News* from the 1890s through the early 1900s and was noted for his coverage of the Chicago World's Fair/Columbian Exposition in 1893 and the World's Fair in Paris in 1900. The first book he illustrated was L. Frank Baum's *Queen Zixi of Ix*, which was serialized in *St. Nicholas Magazine* beginning in 1904. In December of that year, he also illustrated Baum's "A Kidnapped Santa Claus" in *The Delineator* magazine. During the Great Depression, Richardson contributed artwork to the Works Progress Administration.

John Rea Neill (1877-1943) began his drawing career at his high school newspaper in 1984 and later worked as a staff artist at the *Philadelphia North American* newspaper. At the *North American*, he provided illustrations for L. Frank Baum's (under the pseudonym Schuyler Staunton) serialized story "The Fate of a Crown." In 1904 Baum's publisher Reilly and Britton asked Neill to illustrate the forthcoming second Oz book, *The Marvelous Land of Oz*. From that point on, he provided artwork for all the Oz books until Baum's death, then continued with Ruth Plumly Thompson's authorized Oz books, before being designated the "Royal Historian of Oz" and writing and illustrating several of his own Oz books. In total, Neill provided drawings for 30 Oz books.

Walter Hugh McDougall (1858-1938) began working as an artist for America's first illustrated daily newspaper, the *New York Daily Graphic*, in 1876. In the 1880s, while at the *New York World*, he started drawing political cartoons and published one of the first color cartoons in an American newspaper. His work with humorist Bill Nye's newspaper column made McDougall possibly the first syndicated cartoonist. In 1904 and 1905, McDougall illustrated L. Frank Baum's *Queer Visitors from the Marvelous Land of Oz* Sunday comic page.

IF YOU LIKED…

IF YOU LIKED THE SANTA CLAUS STORIES OF L. FRANK
BAUM, YOU MIGHT ALSO ENJOY:

The Complete War of the Worlds
by H.G. Wells and Garrett P. Serviss

A Fantastic Holiday Season
edited by Kevin J. Anderson

A Fantastic Holiday Season 2: The Gift of Stories
edited by Kevin J. Anderson

This book was produced as part of the Publishing MA program for Western Colorado University's Graduate Program in Creative Writing.

OTHER WORDFIRE PRESS TITLES

The Dragon Business
by Kevin J. Anderson

Mythology 101
by Jody Lynn Nye

The Magic Touch
by Jody Lynn Nye

Our list of other WordFire Press authors and titles is always growing. To find out more and to see our selection of titles, visit us at:
wordfirepress.com

CPSIA information can be obtained
at www.ICGtesting.com
Printed in the USA
BVHW030205081220
595167BV00021B/123/J

9 781680 571042